THE
LONE
HUNTER

ALSO BY BETHANY HELWIG

International Monster Slayers:
The Curse of Moose Lake
The Bite of Winter
The Ghosts of Yesteryear
The Dark Whisper
The Brood of Nightmare
The Lone Hunter

~

Darkest Light

INTERNATIONAL MONSTER SLAYERS
A CHARLIE JAEGER NOVELLA

THE LONE HUNTER

BETHANY HELWIG

BRIGHTWAY BOOKS

Copyright © 2019 by Bethany Helwig
Published by Brightway Books, LLC

THE LONE HUNTER, characters, names and related indicia are trademarks of and © Bethany Helwig.
Cover Illustration: Bethany Helwig
All rights reserved.

First Edition: July 2019
ISBN-10: 1-946639-14-1
ISBN-13: 978-1-946639-14-1

For those that suffer in silence.
Let them hear you roar.

Present Day
Part 1

People are idiots. I discovered this unfortunate truth at a young age. They're messy, complicated, and a wild tangle of emotions—but above all, their intelligence seems to border on an inability to even *think*. Common sense is more and more a rare gift than a natural commodity. It makes it difficult for me to even want to try to form relationships when they require so much work. It saves on pain too.

There are the exceptions, of course. When I first met Melody, I found her to be exhaustingly over friendly. I played my usual game of "push away and keep my distance." I thought her kindness to be one of those bland gestures people do when they don't have much else in their head. But Melody was persistent and eventually I discovered her empathy was more intuitive than I ever suspected. Her kindness arose from a sharp intelligence and hid the deadly warrior beneath. Mels was kind because she chose to be, not because a societal norm told her she needed to perform said pleasantries. She knew darkness intimately and in spite of that—or perhaps because of it—she was a gentler person than I probably deserved at the time.

Then there's Phoenix. The first time we met we were at each other's throats. She had touched a nerve that I've been trying to ignore for years but it's as sharp and exposed as ever. I found her sympathy for the werewolves to be naive and ignorant. And she was just as stubborn as I was about it in opposition. It took a while to see her cleverness and the way she throws all of herself into everything she does. Phoenix doesn't take half measures and she'll battle to the last breath for who and what she cares for. It can be annoying at times—like talking to a brick wall— but behind that wall is a force I've never known before. There's resilience I wish I could have. There's undying loyalty I want to earn. She's quick as a whip and cuts like one too when she wants to. And she's funny in a way that makes me want to be in on all her jokes.

But today, reading the letter she left and knowing the rest of my team has abandoned me in this hospital as well, I re-think my stance on exceptions to stupidity. Some things never change. I'll always be left behind or too late.

People are idiots. Perhaps there are no exceptions after all.

The longer I remain in the hospital bed, the more restless I become. I turn Phoenix's pendant over and over in my hand, rubbing my thumb and forefinger over the small metal dragon. She always wears this thing but she left it behind in my care. It's significant, I know that much, but I don't know where she got it or what it means to her. But the fact that she left it for me bodes ill. She honestly doesn't think she's ever going to see me again. The pendant is a token of farewell. Her letter explained that much.

The letter itself is a curled ball resting against my side. It's within easy reach as I keep flattening it out, reading it again, and then crumpling it once more. I've read it so many times now that I almost have it memorized.

Charlie, there's so much I need to tell you but I've never been good with words. I guess I'll get right to it. I'm turning myself in. I'm not going to run from what I am anymore. What that means is I don't know if I'll ever see you again.

I scoff to myself and glare through the window of my room to the falling twilight outside. She's been so adamant about protecting her secrets and what she can do. And now, of all times when I can't do anything about it, she decides to run off without backup. What was she thinking? Melody passed along what transpired between Phoenix and Ashley but I don't care. She shouldn't have gone. Not until I was well enough to protect her. That *idiot*.

Of course, I knew this was coming. Ever since she first exposed her secrets, I knew this day would come. At first I had been angry that she had hidden her abilities for so long.

Now I wish she would have hidden them a while longer.

First off, I want to tell you what a wonderful friend you've been. I was wrong about you in the beginning and I've never been so happy to be so wrong in my life.

I roll my head back onto the pillows, wincing at the movement. I never thought I'd end up shot. I always figured I'd end up clawed to death or ripped to shreds—something incredibly dramatic to save someone's life. To make my life worth something in the end. Honestly, I thought I *was* going to die back there. Not before I made my move. I wasn't thinking about it at that point. All I could think about was a bullet getting put in Phoenix's brain. Nothing else mattered but stopping that bullet.

Then I took that bullet. It was worth it. I was going to go out on a high note by saving the life of a comrade, a friend.

But I survived. And now Phoenix has gone and pitched away that effort like it didn't even matter. Like I don't matter.

Stupid. It's all stupid.

The door to my room opens and a man in a crisp suit enters. Townslee. One of the IMS guards posted outside to keep me safe.

"You've got a phone call," he says and walks over to a phone on the wall to hit a couple buttons before bringing over the wireless receiver to me. He holds it out. "Spartan Ravenspell."

Finally. I take the phone and gingerly bring it up to my ear. "Alona?"

Townslee shuffles back to stand in the doorway with hands clasped behind his back.

"Hey, Charlie. How are you holding up?"

"I'm fine. Ready to get out of here."

"You're not *fine*. You were *shot*."

"I'll heal. Now, are you going to tell me what's going on? I haven't had news for days. What happened when Phoenix went in? And where are you guys? These clowns don't know anything."

Townslee gives me a sour look over his shoulder.

"First, I need you to answer a question for me," Alona says. "What was the last book I recommended to you?"

I stiffen as I realize she's doing a shifter check. I could sound like me and be an impersonator over the phone.

"*Ceremony* by Leslie Marmon Silko." It was one of the books she suggested I put on my ebook reader. I glance to see it resting next to *Pride and Prejudice* on the bedside table. "And what was the last book I recommended to *you*?"

"*The Mote in God's Eye* by Larry Niven." She looses a sigh. "Well, that'll have to be good enough. We can't be sure anymore."

"What are you talking about?"

"The game's changed. I'm calling to warn you."

My gut plummets. "What happened to Phoenix?"

"That's not—we're not in Underground. We're in Paris."

"*Paris?*"

"Get comfortable. I'll walk you through it."

I lay in the hospital bed stunned, my heart hammering in my chest, as Alona explains everything that's happened since they left me here. It ended up that Phoenix didn't turn herself in but it sounds like plenty of other terrible things went down. Hawk working with Genna, the hydra at a secret prison, and worst of all, a new breed of shapeshifters that seem to not only steal appearances but memories.

"We're calling them mimics for now," Alona says. "And we have no idea how far this goes. They could be anyone and anywhere, even deep in the IMS."

"And we have no idea how to spot them?"

"Not yet. Not unless they decide to turn their eyes black. It's the only telltale we know. You could be in danger, Charlie. They might even be expecting us to reach out to you. It's a risk, but considering we're the only ones who know and our situation is . . . precarious, we made the decision to put out the word so at least one other person knows."

The risk is acceptable and necessary, even though it means that anyone in the hospital could be keeping an eye on me to see if my team makes contact. Any nurse, doctor, or janitor could be waiting to pounce if they discover I know about the existence of these "mimics." They've done well at keeping themselves hidden for now. I don't doubt they'll kill anyone that poses a threat to their operation—whatever their endgame is.

"How is everyone? You didn't say, just that you made it out of the prison."

Alona takes a moment too long to answer. "We're okay."

"Now who's the liar?"

"Melody took hydra spit to the face. She's alive but she's lost her left eye and a good chunk of her face. She's being kept sedated."

My heart stutters and the monitor beside me echoes the change. I feel dizzy and my head swims.

Sweet majestics. Mels.

"My arm got messed up and we all have some spit damage. It sucks, but you need to focus on you right now. Don't worry about us. We're survivors."

I should have been there fighting beside them. I could have helped. I could have saved Melody from such a horrible mutilation.

"I'll check back in tomorrow at the same time," Alona says. "We'll stay in touch. If you don't hear from me, then you need to get yourself somewhere safe."

It's clear it doesn't matter that I'm laid up from a gunshot wound. That'll be a nonissue if the mimics come for me. It'll suck but I can do it. I'll have to if it comes to that.

"Stay sharp, Alona."

"You too."

She hangs up and I lower the phone. Townslee takes that as his cue to come fetch it from me to put it back on the receiver before leaving once more.

Mimics. That certainly gives me something to worry about. I'm in terrible condition for any kind of encounter if they do try to snuff me out. But I'm not the only one in danger. If the mimics realize Team Sierra knows about them and survived the prison assault, they'll be hunted. At least they have Phoenix. She's the only safeguard we have against them for the time being until we can discover their tells and weaknesses.

But I don't have a safety net, no magical detector. Any of the nurses could be a mimic come to kill me before I can spread their secret to others. They could be anyone . . . even an IMS guard outside the door. I'm a sitting duck here. It wouldn't be hard for someone to learn where I am and it's not like I'm going anywhere soon. I don't like the thought of that one bit.

I try to push myself up into a sitting position to see how much mobility I have—and quickly slump back onto the pillows. My body's shot—literally and figuratively, but right now the only person I can trust is myself.

I had been used to living on my own, but things have changed of late. I have good people in my life now, people I can count on. Unfortunately, none of them are here. Anxious and tense, I grab my ebook off the bedside table—realizing just how much energy that alone takes out of me—and keep hold of it. It feels good to have something in my hands like a shield. I'm aware how vulnerable I am but having something, even something as small and simple as my ebook reader, makes me feel less so.

When the first nurse comes in to check my vitals and swap out the IV bag, I make forced small talk and ask pointed questions.

"What was your name again?"

The nurse gives me a small smile as she hangs up a fresh IV—at least that's what it looks like. It could be poison for all I know.

"It's Amy. Do you need anything, Charlie?"

"Hey, do you remember what you first told me after I woke up?"

She cocks her head slightly and taps a finger on *Pride and Prejudice* beside me. "I told you how much I liked this book. Why?"

"Just making sure my memory's still intact."

"Do you think you're having memory lapses?" she asks and lays a hand on the railing of my hospital bed. I don't like it. It's a movement to make herself closer to me. My fingers dig into the edges of the ebook reader as I angle it somewhat between me and her. Useless, really, but I do it anyway.

"No, I'm fine," I say. "When do you think I'll be discharged?"

"Don't be in such a rush. You've got a long ways to go in your recovery."

"*When?*"

She blinks and leans back an inch. "We'll keep you for another week and see how you are at that point. After that, count on at least a month and a half of recovery and more than that for physical therapy."

I give a weary sigh. "Fine."

She clears her throat, gives one last smile, and leaves the room.

I know I'm rude. Phoenix and Melody have told me that on plenty of occasions. But I hate small talk. I hate mindless chatter. It's a waste of time and air. No one ever really says anything meaningful. And if being rude manages to save me a few minutes of people trying to chat me up, then I'm fine with that. People are such a pain anyway.

My eyes stay on the clock on the wall and I count out the minutes. Well, there's no ill effects from the IV change so far so I'm assuming it's on the up and up. No one's trying to kill me—yet.

I hate feeling this way. I hate being helpless—and even worse, useless. And right now I'm both. There's nothing I can do for my team. Heck, there's hardly anything I can do for myself. I'm irritated, frustrated, and crabby.

Theo's voice echoes in my head. *Mr. Crabby Pants.*

I roll my eyes even though there's no one here to see. Theo sure can get on my nerves, but he's also become something like a brother. An annoying brother that's somehow become my friend despite myself. I wonder how he is. His roots are in France. Maybe that'll come in handy for the team if they need to make a fast getaway from these mimics.

I hope they're all right. They better not get themselves killed.

Melody must be in a world of pain. I have no business complaining about my own predicament knowing what she's going through. Acid to the face. I close my eyes against the onslaught of mental images, of searing flesh and blood and pain. I sigh heavily through my nose. Sometimes I wish the magical healing spells in books I've read were real. You'd think something like that could exist in our world, but there are only things to speed up the process, more or less. There are no cure alls. There are no phoenix tears or extra lives or golden fleece. Fauns can help speed things along in the body but that's it. Meaning, I'm going to be in this bed a lot longer than I'd like to.

And Melody is never going to be the same.

Guilt begins to chew on my insides. I should have been there with them. I shouldn't have been so reckless. I should have been smarter and got both me and Phoenix out of that house without either of us winding up in the hospital.

There's a light knock on the open door. "Spartan?"

I jerk my head towards the sound, alert and clutching my ebook reader like a shield once again. Agent Townslee waits in the doorway but enters once our eyes meet. Beneath that crisp suit I know he's carrying a bio-mech gun—maybe something more lethal too. That fact stays at the forefront of my mind as he walks to the foot of my bed.

"We just got a call from Director Knox in Underground. We'll be able to transport you to their medical facilities tomorrow."

They're moving me. Transit is always an opportune moment to attack a target. Snuffing me in this hospital could be done by very inconspicuous means too, but maybe the mimics want to make me disappear. Or . . . the IMS just wants to get me to Underground and nothing sinister is happening. Always best to be prepared though.

"Why the transfer now?" I ask.

"They were finally able to clear some room after they got those injured fauns out of there. You know the protocol. Humans stay topside for treatment when the clinic's full in

Underground. You think they can send up fauns or unicorns for treatment at a normal hospital?"

"I thought they extended the space after the attack on Underground last year."

Townslee shrugs. "Yeah, well, there was a big accident about a week ago. I guess some of the repairs were a little shoddy and something blew near the faun fields. A bunch of them were injured. I don't think some made it, actually. Anyway, there's room now. Director Knox would rather have you in the city."

My brow furrows. "Why does the director care?"

The agent lets out a sharp breath, clearly agitated by my string of questions. "Because we're short enough on manpower as it is. If you're in Underground, you won't need guards on duty. Everyone's needed out in the field with those blasted hydra and code blacks." He raps his knuckles on the side railing of my bed. "Get some rest, Spartan. We'll head out tomorrow afternoon, don't worry."

As if I can do anything *but* worry.

Townslee leaves me alone in the room where I consider locking the door—except for the fact that I can't get out of bed. I haven't even attempted to teleport but that would floor me faster than trying to walk.

With my pathetic ebook shield and a weary soul, I wait with alert eyes for the next day to come.

The Past

I can still smell the blood as if it's stuck to my hands and won't wash away despite the rain. I'm drenched from head to toe but I can't feel the cold. I can hardly feel anything at all any more. I don't know where we're going but I don't care. Everything's just . . . numb. I've never been so tired in my life.

"We're almost there." The lady agent waves us on. She came hunting monsters. She'll be leaving soon now that my parents are dead.

Uncle Laurence puts his hand on my shoulder every so often to keep me moving. He doesn't say anything. Just gives me a push to move faster.

Our feet splash through puddles forming on the cement walkway. It's been raining for hours and it feels like we've been walking through it for just as long. We left the agent's car back in the parking lot and have walked through a sort of maze between the mountains to get to this place. My shoes squish with water but I keep moving like some robot in a cartoon.

The lady holds out a hand for us to stop beneath a shelf of rock that shelters us from the rain. "Just a moment."

My eyes follow the back of her raincoat and I realize we've stopped before a pair of huge doors. On either side are black statues that look like lumpy monkeys with wings. I stare at the closest one in a daze and swear that its eyes blink. A little push in my back gets me moving again as the lady opens the big doors that look like part of the stone around them.

Nothing feels real. I'm lost in a dream. At least, that's the only thing that makes sense.

My parents are dead. Two of my grandparents died in a car crash, then one of cancer, the other of old age. I don't have any cousins. No other family except Uncle Laurence. It's just us now. We're the only ones left of our family.

My feet stumble over the smooth stone floor. I keep my eyes down and mindlessly watch water drip off the sleeves of my rain jacket.

"This way," the lady says. My uncle steers me in the right direction again. I try to shrug his hand off my shoulder but he holds on tighter until it hurts. I wince and walk stiffly along. When the lady looks back to make sure we're still following, my uncle's hand instantly falls away from my shoulder.

She stops in front of a big door and holds it open for us. I finally look up to find the walls are made of tan rock like the inside of some cave, bumpy and rough. The agent waits patiently until Uncle Laurence nudges me in the ribs from behind and I walk through the door into the cave-like room beyond. It's not normal, this place. There are torches on the walls to light the small room made of the same rock as the hallway outside. A small fire in a standing iron pit warms the space pleasantly. It's like I'm in the middle of *The Hobbit* by J.R.R. Tolkien. I expect goblins to pop up or maybe even a wizard. But there's a normal table in the middle of the room with normal chairs.

"Can I get you anything to eat or drink?" the lady asks.

She's nice. I like her. And I am a bit thirsty.

"We're fine," Uncle Laurence says. "I just want some answers."

"Of course. I'll need you to wait here for a moment while I go talk to my superior."

"Hurry back."

She nods and shuts the door behind her as she leaves.

I remain standing and stare into the burning fire pit. Uncle Laurence takes a seat, crosses his arms over his chest, and lets out a heavy sigh. He doesn't say anything to me, just taps his fingers impatiently on his jacket.

Tap, tap, tap.

Tap, tap, tap.

BLAM, BLAM, BLAM.

I startle as the memory of those gunshots suddenly sound in my head. My chest heaves and I fight back a sob building in my throat.

Tap, tap, tap.

Tap, tap, tap.

My uncle's fingers continue to drum and all I can hear is him firing a gun over and over again into my mom. Tucking down on myself, I crouch next to the fire pit with my arms wrapped around my legs and my chin on my knees. I don't want to be here. I don't want to be with my uncle. I don't want to be anywhere. I just want my mom and dad.

"Charlie, come here and sit down. You're going to fall face first into that fire."

I shake my head.

"*Charlie*—"

The door creaks open. "Sorry for the wait."

The lady agent returns and immediately walks over to me. She sinks down to my level and holds out a towel.

"Here you go, sweetheart," she says softly. "Let's get you dried up a bit. I can take your jacket."

I don't move. I don't care.

Ever so gently, she unzips my jacket and pulls the sleeves off my arms until I'm free of the soaking thing. She throws the towel over my shoulders and lightly rubs the top of my head with it.

"Do you want to sit in a chair?"

I shake my head.

"Charlie, sit down," my uncle rumbles.

The agent shoots him an angry look and pats my shoulders. "It's okay. You can stay here. Just let me know if you want anything."

"You said you were going to give me answers," my uncle says loudly.

She rises to her feet and takes the chair opposite my uncle. "And you'll get them. But first I need you to fill out some paperwork. I have these forms here about non-disclosure . . ."

The adults continue to talk about things I don't understand and I don't want to. I don't know why we're here or what we're supposed to do. I just want to curl into a ball and disappear. Uncle Laurence's voice raises a few times but I'm not paying attention. The flames dance before my eyes and I wonder how painful it is to be shot. Is it like being burned by a fire? Is it worse? I don't know what that kind of pain feels like. I've fallen out of a tree and hurt my wrist. I've tripped on a sidewalk and scrapped my knees. What's fire feel like?

I find myself reaching out a hand to the brightly glowing flames. My fingers stay at the edge and it gets really hot but it doesn't hurt. I poke a finger into a burning log and immediately jerk away with a cry to clutch my throbbing finger to my chest.

"Charlie!" Uncle Laurence leans towards me from his chair with a frown. "What are you doing over there?"

Tears well in my eyes as I clutch my burned finger beneath the towel.

"What happened? Did you hurt yourself?" the agent asks.

I shake my head. I don't want to get in trouble. It doesn't matter anyway. This pain is my punishment for what I've done.

Everything that's happened is my fault.

"Are you his only relation?" the agent says quietly to my uncle.

"Maybe some distant cousins three times removed but otherwise I'm it. Our family never really kept in touch."

"So I assume you'll be keeping him in your care—"

"Look, sweetheart, that's not . . ."

I watch them out of the corner of my eye as my uncle leans in close to the agent over the table and lowers his voice.

"I'm not father material," he says quietly. "I'm not suited to take care of this kid. Don't you guys have some kind of shelter for kids like this?"

The agent glances at me. "Well, normally those children don't have any relatives left."

"I don't count, not really. He hardly even knows me. I've met him maybe twice in his life? I only came out here because my brother asked me to. The kid would be much better off in someone else's care."

She drums her fingers on the table a few times. "The circumstances for the IMS taking in children are very narrow and specific. We simply don't have the room to be housing normal humans."

"*Normal* humans?"

"Yes, those without magic."

"Humans can have magic?"

"Mr. Jaeger, the best I can do is provide temporary housing through an assistance program."

"What if I became an agent like you?" He raises his voice and his hands curl into fists on top of the table. "There are other monsters than just werewolves, aren't there? I'm sure you can use all the manpower you can get, am I right?"

She doesn't answer immediately but shuffles through some of the papers on the table.

"Am I right?" my uncle repeats.

"You can certainly apply but I'll warn you that people born into the life or who grow up in facilities like this are far more likely to be chosen as agents. There's a good chance you won't make the cut."

"I'll take my chances. I want to learn how to kill the things like that piece of trash that killed my brother."

"*Mr. Jaeger.*" The agent's eyes dart to me.

I return my gaze to the fire and wish I could throw myself

in. For what seems like a long time, the only sound is the crackling of the logs amid the flames.

The door to the room creaks open and a man says, "Agent Mason, might I have a word?"

"Draco." The agent shoots up to her feet, her chair screeching across the rough floor. "Of course, sir."

I don't even turn around as I hear the pair of them leave and shut the door behind them. My uncle doesn't say anything and neither do I. The tip of my finger pulses with pain and I peek at it underneath the towel. It's red and the skin has risen with a blister. If Mom was here, she would have been in a panic. She always freaked out when I got hurt. Dad would just say I need to be tough or might even get mad at me. I stopped showing either of them when I got hurt. I'd try to patch it up myself just so they wouldn't look at me the way they did.

The door opens again.

"What's going on?" Uncle Laurence demands.

No one responds but someone walks forward to stand directly before me. My eyes travel up a black suit to a man staring intently at me. There's something in his eyes that makes me nervous, even though he doesn't look scary. Just a regular person. He holds out a hand.

"Come," is all he says.

I swallow and take his hand. He leads me out of the room away from my uncle and past the agent waiting outside. We walk hand in hand down a rough stone hallway until we reach a bubbling fountain in a shallow pool. The man takes a seat on the rim of the pool and motions for me to do the same. I sit down and watch the intricate fountain springing out of the mouth of a mermaid statue. What is this place?

"What's your name, child?" the man asks gently.

"Charlie."

"My name's Draco. I'm here to help you."

"Can you bring my parents back?"

"No."

I sniffle and run the back of my hand under my nose. "Then you can't help me."

"I can, however, give you the power to protect yourself and others from a similar fate. You could save other children from losing their parents, but I need your help. Would you like that? Could you help me?"

"How?"

"I need you to tell me exactly what happened to your mother."

Mom. I remember the fur and fangs and horrible sound as my father tried to breath with blood bubbling out of his torn throat. I shrink in on myself and pull my knees in to my chest.

"I know it's hard," he says gently. "But I know you're brave. You proved that when you agreed to help Agent Mason. I need you to be brave once more. Tell me how everything started."

I keep my eyes on the bubbling fountain. "My mom said we were going on a trip. It was a secret and I couldn't tell Dad. I packed my stuff and we drove into the mountains."

It was sort of fun in the beginning. Mom bought me ice cream and got me whatever I wanted. Her phone kept ringing and she got mad when it did, but otherwise we were happy.

"Then what happened?" Draco asks.

The memory becomes clear before my eyes as if I'm there again. "We got a hotel room then went out so Mom could get some money. I was in the car. She went outside." I suck in a sharp breath. Her screams and the terrible snarls of that night echo in my head. "I . . . I don't know what happened next. She got hurt and went to the hospital."

That's what I told my uncle and my dad—not the truth. They wouldn't have believed it. It becomes hard to see, hard to breath. It's all my fault.

Draco sets a hand between my shoulder blades and rubs in small circles. "It's okay. What happened? What did you see?"

I tuck in even tighter, arms wrapped around my legs and chin tucked down.

"Are you going to tell my uncle?" I whisper.

"Not if you don't want me to. It can be our little secret. I'll protect you. I only want the truth, that's all."

When he says it, I believe him.

"There was a wolf," I say in a hushed voice. "It came out of nowhere and attacked Mom. She ..." Blood and screams and terror. I press my hands to my ears as if I can drown out the noise inside my head and squeeze my eyes shut tight. "It bit her then ran away. She was hurt really bad. We were going to go to the hospital but then—"

The unthinkable happened.

"She turned into a wolf," Draco finishes for me.

I nod. She ran off and I was terrified. I went back to the hotel, unsure what to do. That's when Dad and Uncle Laurence showed up.

"What did the wolf look like that bit your mother?" Draco asks.

"I don't know."

"Was it all black?"

"Maybe. It was dark."

He pats me on the shoulder. "I am sorry this happened to you, Charlie."

"Did I help?"

"You did. Now I'll do as I promised. Pull your arm out of your jacket."

Confused, I do as I'm told and pull my left arm free of my raincoat. Draco pushes up the sleeve of my shirt. Goosebumps rise on my bare arm as he presses three fingers to my skin. Suddenly the tips of his fingers feel hot and he drags them down from near my shoulder to partway down my arm. When he removes his hand, there are three silver streaks left behind on my skin that glow faintly.

"I just gave you a rare gift," Draco says and carefully pulls my sleeve back down over the strange mark. "As you grow, power will grow with you. Soon you may discover you can do things other humans cannot."

"Like what?"

"I cannot say. It is different for every person who receives this gift. But you will make it your own and it will give you the strength to protect yourself and those around you. You are special, Charlie. You are Blessed. Do not abuse your abilities when they come. Use them for the good of the world."

Abilities? Like a superhero? I massage my arm as the heat fades. I don't feel any different. At least I don't think I do.

"What now?"

"Now you rest and we take care of you. We can teach you how to harness your gifts when they develop. You will never be alone. You will always have a place here."

Present Day
Part 2

I wake the following morning and take it as a good sign that no one's tried to kill me yet. Otherwise, my would-be murderers are incredibly incompetent if they can't take me out when I'm asleep. Not that I meant to fall asleep, but it's a little hard not to when you've got a hole in your chest. Actually, I'm surprised I managed to stay awake as long as I did.

A short while later the nurse—I mean *Amy*—comes in to check my vitals and see what I want for breakfast. I keep my eyes on her the entire time but she doesn't do anything suspicious. I try to decline food but she insists that I eat something at least. This is a precarious time for me, she says. I need to heal up, she says. Yeah, yeah. I also don't need poisoned food. That's far too easy. Amy—ugh, I hate using first names with people I don't know—tries to carry on some small talk as if I need my mind taken off my circumstances. No thanks.

"Well, just sit tight," she says. "I'll be right back with breakfast, Charlie."

I don't respond. She exits with a smile.

Once I'm alone, I mumble, "It's Jaeger."

People always get too familiar. They think they know you or try to be friendly by using first names or nicknames or chatting you up like you're the best of pals. The truth is, I don't care. I don't care to get friendly or familiar and it irritates me when I encounter people who do. They *don't* know me. They *don't* know what I've been through. And honestly, I don't care to share.

Two battered yet happy faces pop into my head—the redhead twins sitting on either side of my hospital bed in Underground, browsing through the books Melody brought me. I hadn't been pleasant towards them—the same way I treat everyone—but they were there swapping jokes and including me in their inner circle. Their "island of besties."

A hollow ache settles in my chest next to the gunshot wound.

Amy returns with a tray of food. "Here we go." She swings a table about that slips over the top of my bed so it's all within easy reach. "Do you need help at all? Do you think you can grip things or is the pain still limiting your movement?"

I do a test run and slowly bring up my right arm to grab the cup of chocolate pudding.

Then clearly remember Hawk stealing mine from the same memory that I was just thinking about. What is it with hospitals and pudding?

With my other hand, I manage to lift the provided spoon but there's a throb of pain deep in my chest that radiates up through my body. I nudge the pudding towards the nurse.

"Take a bite and let me know what you think?" I ask. "I don't trust hospital food."

"I really shouldn't."

"I've been shot. Indulge me."

She levels a frown at me but then picks up the spoon and takes a small scoop. After a quick taste, she says, "Tastes fine to me."

"Great. What about the toast?"

"You want me to sample all of your food?"

"That'd be great."

Amy sighs. "Charlie, I—"

"Please," I say quietly and roll my lips. I hate being at someone else's mercy or having to ask for help. "Please, just…"

She stares at me for a solid five seconds before ripping off a corner of the toast, taking the smallest orange slice, and carefully tipping a few drops of milk into her open mouth. Then she tucks the used spoon into her pocket and lowers her eyes.

"I'll get you a fresh one," she says and makes for the door.

"Thank you," I say towards her back.

That's when I notice Townslee standing in the shadow of the doorway watching. He moves aside to let Amy through then disappears himself. Well, the food might not be poisoned, but I just got a bad feeling.

A minute passes before she returns with a spoon—silently this time as if I've spooked her. Good. She ought to be spooked. I eat my breakfast and realize, to no surprise, that I'm famished. Light-headed, actually. That's not good. I need to replenish my strength if I'm going to be able to defend myself. After chewing on the inside of my cheek for a good five minutes, I press the button to summon Amy to have her fetch more food. This time she takes a few quick bites of everything and gives me this sort of look that reminds me eerily of Phoenix when she's annoyed.

I wonder how Phoenix is doing considering everything that's happened.

My fingers crawl along the sheets until I find her letter again and curl it into my fist. Her words rise to haunt me again.

You've always had my back, even when I didn't realize it. And when I didn't deserve it.

Well, I don't have her back now, do I? She's halfway around the world and getting into who knows what kind of trouble. What if the mimics already know what she's capable of? That they know to target her to keep themselves hidden? That nasty thought twines around my resolve.

I need to get out of this hospital.

But I wait. That's what Alona said to do. Wait for her call.

The morning passes and I take my time ever so slowly moving my arms and attempting to move my legs to test my range of motion. It's pretty shoddy.

Then noon comes and another meal with an awkward moment with Amy.

Outside my window the light wanes and the shadows grow long without a phone call.

Townslee swings by a few times to let me know they're waiting on transportion to take me to Underground. It's taking longer than expected. We're going to wait around a while longer. The more he assures me of that, the less safe I feel. Are they really waiting for a ride? Or waiting for another phone call to come in?

Twilight comes.

And goes.

Every time I hear a phone ring softly in the distance at the nurse's station, I perk up, but no one comes with a call. Night begins to fall. What's taking Alona so long? I give it an hour. Then an hour and a half before I accept something has happened to the team.

Meaning I need to get out of here before I'm next.

Tucking Phoenix's pendant underneath my hospital gown and grabbing my ebook, I ease myself to the edge of the mattress. It's a slow process of swinging my legs over the side until I'm sitting upright. I'm okay though. Pain is temporary anyway. I press the button to summon Amy.

"Going somewhere?" she asks when she enters the room.

"Could you grab a wheelchair? I want to go sit by the big bay windows overlooking the road."

"Are you sure? It's getting late."

"I'm sure."

With a bob of her head, she disappears and returns with a wheelchair. I ignore her offered arm, rise on my own unsteady legs, and settle into the wheelchair with my ebook reader in my lap.

"I can take it from here," I say.

"Feeling a bit cooped up?"

"Yes."

I grasp both wheel handles and maneuver myself about. Amy, however, walks along beside me down the hall past Townslee and the other guards. I can feel their eyes on my back and then hear their footsteps following. This is going to be tricky. If I'm going to make this work, several things will need to line up. First, I'll need a clear exit and those big bay windows are going to be my best bet. They overlook a lot of cars, any of which I could port right into the driver's seat—but then I'd need to have access to keys or be able to hot wire it before anyone could run out after me. Next, I'd need to have enough distance or barriers between me and everyone else. Leaving them trapped back in the building is my best option by using a window to my advantage to separate myself. Third, I'll need some kind of supply to get myself on my way. The team left my civilian clothes here along with my wallet so I'll have means for funds—but I'll have to swap cards for cash quick so I can't be tracked. Pain meds would be good and a stack of bandages. Then the final step would be finding myself a safe place to lie low until I can figure out my next step.

Amy walks silently beside me and remains close as I roll to a stop before the wide windows to have a look at what's available. I like having a plan in place before action when I can. When I jump the gun too early, things tend to not end well.

Under the lights of the hospital and street lamps, I make out a small selection of vehicles I could port into.

I'm in the midst of calculating risks and variables when Amy sits on the window sill next to me.

"Are you waiting for someone?" she asks.

I ignore her comment and keep on playing different scenarios in my head.

"What happened to your friends that were here earlier? They never left your side and then all of a sudden they just disappeared. They haven't been back for days—"

"And pointing that out really makes me feel so much better, thank you for that."

She exhales sharply through her nose and crosses her arms. "I'm just trying to help. I was going to say, do you need me to contact anyone for you? I'm sure your friends would come back in a heartbeat if you asked."

It clicks together in my head. There's a reason I'm not dead yet. If Alona didn't call today, it's because the team was either killed or on the run. If the latter, I would be the enemy's best chance of finding them—using me to get to them. They would come if I needed them, thick-headed as they are, even if I'm not worth the effort.

And Amy's questions have quickly turned her into suspect number one for being a mimic.

"I need to go to the bathroom," I mutter and wheel about.

Amy shadows me.

Townslee and the other agents are hanging back in the hallway to remain within eyesight. When they see me coming, Townslee walks up to meet me.

"I just got a call from our people in the Twin Cities," he says. "A transport should be arriving here in about ten minutes to bring you down."

Whether this transport is a trap or legit, I can't tell, but this fight is starting to take its toll. I hate being in the dark. I want answers. I need some kind of defense to protect myself.

"He's not ready to be discharged," Amy says over my shoulder. "And he shouldn't be moving around too much either."

If she is a mimic, that's exactly what she would want.

Townslee's eyes shift to me before he squares off with the nurse. "It's not a discharge. He's heading to a facility better suited to treat him."

I wheel myself between the pair and mutter, "I need to go to the bathroom first."

Making a beeline for my room, I immediately go to the

closet that has my belongings so I can grab them to flee. The closet's empty.

"I've already loaded your stuff," Townslee says from the doorway.

"Great." I look at him over my shoulder. "Are you planning on following me into the bathroom too? Or can I take care of my business without a guard?"

He gives me a flat stare but takes a step back. He's still closer than I'd like. I wheel into the bathroom only to remember there's no window in here for me to use to port out. A sigh escapes me as I realize I'll need to do this the hard way.

A minute later I exit the bathroom to find Townslee and the rest of the guards waiting for me. The lead agent waves me on. There's really only one option left to me now. I need to get my stuff then make a fast exit. The second I clear the door of my room, one of the guards takes up the duty of pushing and steering my wheelchair. It puts my teeth on edge losing even that small amount of control. I'm on a slippery slope here.

I'm led like a prisoner to the rear exit where an ambulance sits waiting for me outside the doors. The main lights outside the door are off and I hear some of the nurses at the station behind me wondering about it and calling someone to come check it out. If things felt suspicious before, now I know something's wrong. With the lights off, it's hard for me to see far in the distance. The furtherest I could port is partway across the parking lot. It's as if someone knows exactly how to contain me. I need line of sight to teleport somewhere.

"We've got a bed set up for you," Townslee says and gestures an arm to the open doors of the ambulance. Indeed there is a hospital bed ready for me. I can't help but wonder if there are straps that come with it to tie me down. "Should make the trip a bit more comfortable."

"Where's my stuff?" I ask.

"In a duffle up front."

"I want my cell phone."

"It's in there. Let's get you settled first, okay? Come on."

Two of the men pull the bed out of the ambulance and set it low to make it easier for me to get on. Townslee grabs my elbow without warning and tugs me up out of the wheelchair. I sway on my feet, one hand desperately clutching my ebook reader.

A voice calls out behind us. "Wait!"

Amy jogs out from the hospital and straight to me. Something glints in her hand. The next second Townslee shoves me back into the wheelchair and grabs Amy's hand just as she attempts to skewer me with a loaded syringe. My entire chest gives a painful jolt and the wheelchair rolls back a couple feet as the two struggle. Shouts and other bodies add to the chaos. Then as quick as it happens, it ends. Amy's flattened to the ground with two agents on her back.

"Get him out of here!" Townslee shouts to the other two and gestures to the ambulance. I'm lifted by both elbows this time and hoisted onto the waiting bed. I keep my eyes on Amy as she lies spitting angry and attempting to struggle away. I had an inkling there was something fishy about her but she played her part well. If I hadn't been warned by Alona, I never would have known a shapeshifter was in my midst.

The bed is wheeled into the back of the ambulance and the doors shut on the scene outside as the agents begin handcuffing the mimic. I guess they were coming to kill me after all and made a run of it once it looked like I was slipping through their fingers.

We don't head out immediately. One of my protectors turns on the light in the back and sits on the bench beside me. The other chats with the driver up front.

"You okay?" the man beside me asks. I never bothered to learn his name. He gestures to the hand I have tightly pressed against my wound.

I quickly remove my hand and fight back a grimace despite the pain. "I'm fine."

Moments later, the rear doors open again and Townslee hops in to join us, making it pretty cramped.

"Let's hit the road," he says. "A cleanup crew will pick up the others."

The engine rumbles to life and we begin our journey away from the hospital.

Townslee sits perched close to my side. "Do you have any idea what that was about?"

"Maybe it was one of the lamia's friends trying to finish me off."

"Well, that girl was no lamia, and she passed the shape-shifter test."

"And she can only be one of those two options?"

He tilts his head to the side. "Okay, I take it you have a theory?"

"No theory. Just stating the obvious. If she's not one of the two, then there's another explanation. There always is."

"What, you think there are *other* monsters working with the lamia?"

I roll my eyes. "I want my cell phone."

Townslee gestures to one of the men over my shoulder. I try to look in the same direction to see through the front windshield but the view is blocked by one of the guards who hands over my phone. I check it in the hopes of seeing a missed call from Alona letting me know they're okay. Instead, a single text message pops up from an unknown number with a single word.

RUN.

I immediately turn the phone off and face down so the others don't see the message. Whether that message was to warn me about the mimic posing as the nurse or not, I need to make myself scarce. And that means escaping from these IMS agents—if that's what they truly are. The ambulance rumbles along as I remain sitting up on the hospital gurney considering my options.

"You sure you don't want to rest?" Townslee asks and gestures to the bed. I shake my head. He sighs and shifts to one side so the gun holstered at his waist is clearly visible—and not a bio-mech gun at that. "I suppose you'd rather run then like that mysterious text suggested."

Our eyes meet. I find his to be completely black, whites and all.

Mimic.

They're done playing games because they know I'm on to them.

An arm wraps around me from behind and the sharp stab of a needle goes into the side of my neck. The mimic raises his gun to aim at my chest but doesn't fire.

He should have if he wanted to stop me.

I vanish.

Right out of the man's arms and next to the mimic on the bench. When I appear my hand is already on his sidearm and I immediately aim the barrel down to shoot his foot. He lets out a roar of pain before I send an elbow to his face. I shoot through the man that stuck me with the syringe—still dangling from the side of my neck currently—and hit the driver. The ambulance makes a sharp turn that flings everybody to the far side of the vehicle.

Wheezing and consumed with pain, I stumble to the rear of the ambulance, shoot the third kidnapper that tries to stop me, and fling open the rear door. I'd like to make a safe jump out the back but the vehicle makes another jerky movement with a loud screech and I tumble awkwardly out the open door.

I fall hard on pavement where I roll and roll until every part of me is scraped up and bleeding. My body lays in shock and my lungs refuse to expand for a solid seven seconds. Out of the corner of my eye I see the ambulance careen off the road and roll into a dark ditch.

When I'm finally able to breathe again, I still can't move. My body is too broken to make an effort to flee.

There's movement from the ambulance lying on its side. I don't have much time.

We've crashed on a mostly deserted road surrounded by pine trees. The only visible thing in the distance is a lonesome house and barn, a floodlight illuminating both. I have a clear line of sight to the front sloping roof of the house.

My vision starts to blur and it's difficult to focus. I manage to bring up one shaking hand to my neck to find the syringe is gone but the needle and bits of glass are imbedded in my skin. Whatever they gave me is pulling me under—that, and the amount of blood I've lost considering how it's soaking through my clothes. I have to move.

This is going to hurt.

Gathering myself for one final push, I vanish.

In a whirl of agony, I slam onto the roof of the house and just about fall off.

This can't be good for my recovery.

The world tilts on its axis and everything spins while I try to keep a grip on the gun in my hand. It's impossible to hoist it to aim. It's impossible to keep my eyes open any longer. Darkness and pain drag me into nothingness.

The last thing I hear is Townslee yelling, "You can't escape, Charlie! And no one's coming to save you!"

The Past

I stare into the endless depths of the great Pit before my feet. The darkness within seems to swallow up everything around it. I overheard someone say it goes half a mile deep. During the day, gryphons with golden feathers, brown fur, and sharp beaks and talons fly in and out of the void. They practice fighting and flying together. Pillars line the chasm along a curved stone lip to protect people from falling in. But here, on this ledge, is where the gryphons enter.

Where there's currently no one at all but me.

I've seen them practice. The gryphons stretch out their wings and limbs, walk like giant freakish cats to the very edge, and then . . . fall. There's really no leap or great lift of their wings. They simply drop. Of course, they rise up seconds later on their great wings and circle until the rest of their friends join them.

I wonder what it would be like to fall. What would it feel like if I just put my foot over the edge and let go? How long would it take for me to reach the bottom?

Would the pain be any worse than what I feel in my chest every day? Would the screaming thoughts finally be silent?

It would be so easy. Just one step. A slight lean forward.

I teeter on the edge with the void staring back at me as if it's alive. Calling me. Taunting me.

"What are you doing here, boy?"

I startle and tip towards that darkness. My stomach leaps up into my throat as the movement starts to take me. But then steadfast talons grab the back of my shirt and pull me away from the yawning mouth. It takes a few seconds to be able to breath again. I almost fell in.

Those strong talons tear into my shirt and drag me back a few steps before letting go. A towering gryphon stalks around from behind to put itself between me and the edge. Despite its large talons on its bird-like front legs, and the massive claws on its lion hind legs, the gryphon hardly makes a sound. It's feathers—that cover head, wings, and the front half of its body—are a fiery golden color. Its back half could have come from a mountain lion had its tail not ended in the same fiery feathers. Bright, green eyes pin me where I stand. Two long tufts of feathers—like odd ears on either side of its head—lay flat in irritation.

It's beautiful. It's terrifying. It's huge.

"You're the boy that came with the trainee from Colorado, aren't you?" The gryphon has an odd sort of voice. Deep with clicks from its beak.

I nod.

"What were you doing just now?"

My gaze falls to my toes. "Just looking."

"This area is off limits."

I'm so stupid. Stupid, stupid, *stupid*.

He shouldn't have caught me. He should have just let me fall.

"What's your name?" the gryphon asks.

My lower lip trembles and I'm so angry with myself that I don't respond.

"I am General Bakari," the gryphon says. "I'm the protector of everyone who resides in Dreamland. That includes you. This is no place for children."

"There's no place for me," I mumble and keep my eyes down.

"Nonsense. My people believe that everyone has a purpose in life, they just need to seek it out. Everyone belongs somewhere. Maybe for you, it's not here in this moment, but you will find your place."

I run the back of my hand under my nose. "What if where I'm supposed to be . . . what if it doesn't exist anymore? Then what do I do?"

"You will always belong somewhere. Your life will continue to have meaning even if one fate is taken from you. There is always another path." He shakes out his wings, buffeting me a bit by the force of it. "Come with me, child."

One of his wings drapes around my back and pulls me in to his side. His feathers are glossy against my skin. I rest a hand on his side and clutch a bundle above his odd bird leg.

"Not too tightly," Bakari says.

We walk along, his talons hardly making a sound and my

shoulder bumping into his wing every so often. This is the closest I've been to one of the gryphons. There are so many things
to look at—the shimmering gold in the feathers, the transition
from feather to fur, the tufts for ears, the strange way they walk
with two different kinds of legs. Yet, somehow, all the pieces fit
together. Bakari is big enough that an adult could ride on his
back with a saddle like a horse.

"Can I sit on your back?" I ask, taken by the impulse to do so.

Bakari comes to a sudden halt and snaps his beak. I flinch
away from him. He swivels his head low to bring one large eye
level with me.

"Never ask a gryphon such a thing. It is very rude."

"I'm sorry," I whisper.

"Do not mistake us for common beasts. Such is the folly
of humans. But you're not a normal human, are you? Are you,
boy?" I shake my head. "Then do not act like one. Come."

He continues to walk and I shuffle along beside him
hunched and ashamed.

Together we travel the long stone hallways through
Dreamland into the gryphon aerie. There are pictures carved
into the walls of gryphons and dragons fighting monsters, centaurs and fauns in armor, humans throwing spears at a giant
lizard with three heads, and so on. Curiosity burns my insides.
I want to ask who made the carvings, what each of them are
about, if all those creatures are real, but the last time I asked
someone—my uncle—he told me I was being annoying. I guess
I'm always annoying.

My eyes linger on the carvings and I almost trip when
Bakari makes a turn without me noticing. We enter a hallway
I've never been down before with torches along the walls. My

heart gives a great leap when I see eyes peering at me from out of the flickering flames.

"Mister Bakari—" I gasp.

"It's general, boy. And yes. The fires are alive."

"How?"

Bakari halts and lifts his beak towards the closest torch. The flames shift and two eyes appear to stare back. A tiny hand reaches out and taps the gryphon's beak before making an odd sound sort of like a cat purring.

"They're fire sprites. One of the four types of elemental beings in the world. No one is exactly sure where they came from, only that they tend to gather where magic is plentiful, where it saturates the very earth and air."

"Are they dangerous?"

"Anything can be dangerous. But they are not hostile, no. They will not harm you. It's best not to antagonize them, however. It would be like kicking a hornet's nest."

He brings his wing in around me once again to pull me along. Glowing eyes follow us from each of the torches on the walls. How is something like that even alive? What keeps them alive? Do they eat wood? Can they talk? Are they as smart as people or more like wild animals?

I hardly notice when we pass out of the hallway and into a large, open room.

"Perhaps this is a better place to spend your time than the edge of an abyss," Bakari says.

My breath catches in my throat as I lay my eyes on the sight before me. We've reached a sort of cave but it's not cold or clammy or dark. It's full of more torches to illuminate the walls of orange, gold, and black striped stone. They aren't shaped like the hallways with straight lines and carvings. These sort of flow like frozen waves, bending and twisting around the bookshelves and tables that fill the room. Winding pillars stand here and there dispersed throughout. And everywhere there are books—big ones with leather covers, small delicate ones, and those with pages colored by age and bent with use.

A library.

Mom used to read to me. I love reading. Dad used to say I should play outside more.

I wrap my arms around myself and walk slowly to the closest table where there's a book lying open with a picture of a gryphon.

"The great thing about libraries," Bakari says, "is that they contain both the past and the future, the known and the unknown, and you can go anywhere you want without going anywhere at all. Amongst the pages you'll find the unexpected and exactly what you're looking for."

I blink up at him. "How long can I stay in here?"

"For as long as you like. Take care, young one." The gryphon starts to walk away.

"Charlie."

He pauses and looks over a folded wing. "Pardon?"

"My name's Charlie."

Bakari tilts his head to the side and almost looks like he's smiling.

"Welcome to Dreamland, Charlie."

Present Day
Part 3

*B*eep. *Beep.*

Beep. Beep.

What an annoying . . .

Wait. That's a familiar beat. A heart rate monitor.

Ow. *Ow.* Why does everything have to hurt?

Opening my eyes is a struggle. But I have to know where I've ended up.

It's not a well lit room. Just one bulb overhead illuminates me. The rest of the space fades into inky blackness. It's unsettling. There's nothing to see except the bed I'm in, an IV bag hooked up to my arm, a table at my side with the heart rate monitor, and next to it a number of bloodied surgical utensils amongst piles of red-soaked gauze.

Well, I'm alive. There's that.

And now completely at the mercy of the mimics.

"Try not to move too much, dear," a woman's voice says from the shadows. "It took considerable effort on my part to stitch you back together."

I swallow past my dry throat. "What do you want from me?"

"An answer to a simple question."

"I'll never talk."

"Except you have, in multiple instances now, so clearly you *are* capable. So answer me this . . ."

A women steps into view beneath the dim light. She has a narrow sort of face nearly swallowed up by the long, sweeping curls of her hair. There's a predatory movement to her as she stalks forward to the end of my bed. Her eyes are narrowed and glint with the promise of my demise if I test her. She stops at my feet and holds aloft a silver pendant—Phoenix's necklace.

"Why do you have this when I clearly gave it to Phoenix Mason?" she asks sounding rather bitter.

I don't know if this is actually the person who gave Phoenix that pendant. Anyone could say that. Doesn't make it true. Heck, Phoenix has never said who gave it to her, never hinting at gender, age, or anything to even give me a clue. Then again, how does she even know the pendant belongs to Phoenix?

She waits impeccably still but her eyes continue to glint. This is a person I don't want to trifle with, but that's about my only option really.

"Okay, I'll talk," I say. "To say I'm not going to tell you what you want to know."

Her eyes narrow even more and she stalks around to the side of my bed. "That would be foolish as I am the one keeping you alive."

"It doesn't matter. I'm as good as dead."

"Is that so? I thought Phoenix's teammate would be a bit more concerned about saving his comrades than sulking with a gunshot wound."

My heart thunders in my chest and I look away.

"So you *do* want to help them," she says. "But are unwilling to talk to me. I suppose you consider yourself a prisoner. You certainly don't trust me and think I will take your life once I get what I want. Am I correct so far?"

I don't respond. She starts to circle around behind me.

"I suppose I should offer some proof of who I am and my intentions."

There's an odd sound behind me and when she comes around to my other side, she's no longer human in appearance. A scaled, triangular head slips past followed by a long, thin body of glistening green scales. Claws click quietly on the hard floor and the brilliant frill around her face fans out for a moment before settling flat against her body. She walks around the bed to take a seat at my feet, a shiver traveling down the sharp spikes lining her spine. A terrene dragon.

I'm pretty sure the mimics can't do *that*.

So . . . not a shapeshifter, not a mimic. Clearly a dragon. Phoenix's pendant is a dragon. Could be a coincidence. Might not be.

But still . . . how can I simply *trust* her?

"Not what you were expecting?" she says, a slight hiss to her words.

"No. I'm deciding if that's a good thing or not."

She grins to reveal her sharp teeth. "You're a clever, paranoid boy. I think we'll get along splendidly."

"Depends on who you are."

"You may call me Scholar. I owe you thanks for assisting me two years ago. Without your help, Phoenix would not have been able to get past the barrier around my home to come to my rescue. I'm not used to needing aid, but I certainly appreciate it when it is warranted."

So she's *that* dragon. The mysterious dragon the lamia wanted to kill, the selkies were adamant we protect, and that Phoenix nearly died for in that mansion. I nearly died too, but I didn't do it for this random stranger. Not for her.

For someone else who could very well be in grave danger at this very moment. Headstrong, foolish, temperamental, and always getting herself in trouble. And one of the few people that I honestly trust without a doubt. I have no idea where she is now.

But I need to deal with this dragon first.

"Okay. Maybe you are who you say you are. Convince me so I can decide if I need to kill you or not. I have places to be."

She lets out a throaty huff. "Yes, by all means. Struggle away and bleed to death on the way to your destination. Or, instead, make an ally with the dragon that saved you from those beasts pretending to be IMS agents." A tremor goes through her frill and she crosses her forelegs over each other, head held high. "As for the convincing, I'd like to think I've already made progress by saving your life. I am offering you sanctuary here until you are well enough. I will answer your questions. And, in turn, I hope you will help me rescue Phoenix from whatever fool's errand she has run off on."

"How do you know it's a fool's errand?"

"Because she left my beacon with you," she says and gives a low growl. "Idiot child. She's going to get herself killed."

"She's not an idiot," I say hotly.

"Live as long as I have, dear, and you realize most people are idiots. I do hope you're one of the exceptions. Alona seems to think you are."

I blink.

"Don't be mistaken in thinking Phoenix is my only friend," she says. "Alona has been giving me progress updates, including Phoenix's ill-advised reveal of her full capabilities."

It becomes plain then who this Scholar really is. Phoenix kept referencing a mysterious "friend" that advised her to hide her abilities and to be wary of the IMS. If I recall correctly, Scholar has secrets of her own that Phoenix wasn't willing to give up—to keep the team safe. Why? What does this terrene know that's so monumental that her secrets could endanger a Spartan team?

"So you'll answer any of my questions?" I ask. She bobs her serpentine head. "Why did you warn Phoenix against Draco?"

Her tail twitches like a cat's when watching prey. "It seems the girl revealed even more than I thought—more than she had a right to."

"She protected your secrets as best as she could. I'm the one that—"

I swallow, my throat suddenly dry. I can still remember the look on her face when I hounded her about her abilities, cornered her in the Osprey so she couldn't flee, and demanded answers. She was terrified and . . . heartbroken. I did that. I didn't care or think about it at the time. I was mad she hid something so serious. It brought up a surge of anger. I've been conditioned by trust being broken, no thanks to my uncle. I regret that now.

"Draco told me to keep an eye on her," I say quietly. "Report anything out of the ordinary."

Her slit eyes narrow even more and her lips pull back to reveal her teeth again. "What did you do?"

I stare the angry dragon down. "Nothing. I didn't tell him anything. So you tell me what Draco wants with Phoenix."

She flicks her tongue out like a snake and readjusts her position on the floor. "A means to an end, that end being finding me. To kill me, I assume. Possibly extract a bit of revenge through torture first. It's unclear what his *exact* intentions are. I don't intend on asking him personally to avoid learning the specifics firsthand."

"And that's supposed to make me trust you . . . why?"

"It's beside the point. As for his specific intentions regarding Phoenix, she was to guide him to me. If he could not make that use of her, he most certainly has been keeping an eye on her with suspicions of what she's capable of. He's right, of course, but his method of handling her abilities would destroy her."

The thought of it puts me on edge. "So what use do *you* have for her? You obviously have an interest."

"We all have our ailments," she says slyly and her tail twitches some more. "Phoenix is a potential cure for such ailments. I intend to protect her as long as I am able. At the moment, that means finding out where she's gone this time and why she left my pendant behind. It was a means to find her whenever she was in danger. It saved her life once already."

I nod slowly. "You were the one who tipped off Alona about the lamia in Moose Lake."

"I was. Then I sensed death closing in once again, but when I arrived I found you instead. Imagine my fury."

Heat builds in my face. "I'm used to being a disappointment. I won't take it personally."

But what she says makes sense. I'm beginning to believe she truly is who she says.

"Where has she gone?" she asks.

I sigh and wince at the pain it brings. My palm settles over the worst of it where a bullet went through me. "She was going to turn herself in. She was tired of hiding."

Scholar looses a sharp snarl that makes me jump. "Alona should have informed me."

"She didn't go through with it," I say. "She and the rest of the team ran off to France before she could tell Director Knox." I relay what Alona told me of what transpired once they got to France—of hydra and mimics and blowing up a prison.

The dragon gets up to pace back and forth. Her tail hits the wall with a heavy thud and scraping sound each time she makes a turn in the room that's clearly too small for her.

"Alona attempted to contact me," she growls. "But I was too busy tracking down Epsilon and missed her call." In a string of snarls and hisses, she rants in Draconic I can't understand. After many turns pacing and what I'm pretty sure is swearing on her part, she eventually slows and quiets. She taps a claw on the floor and swivels to face me again.

"You thought I was one of these mimics."

I nod.

"So those beasts hunting you in the skin of IMS agents were mimics."

I nod again.

"Echidna has been busy," she mutters. "Such movement on her part is alarming. She has not mobilized in such a fashion in five hundred years. Her forces are planning to strike first to catch the world unaware. It is up to us to stop her."

"We need to discover their weaknesses before it's too late. We need a mimic."

She nods. "We need a mimic. How do you feel about being bait?"

"Willing."

"I'd say that's the best response I've received to date."

I raise an eyebrow. "How often do you ask people that question? And should I be worried?"

She waves a dismissive paw at me. "You'll be safe. However, before we attempt such an endeavor, you must rest and heal."

"We can't wait that long."

"How have you survived for so long with such disregard for your own life?" She huffs through her flared nostrils. "You will *heal*. You will *rest*. You are to be bait but you are not to be supper. I dare say Phoenix would never speak to me again otherwise."

"But—"

"I am aware of the time-sensitive nature of our goals, dear," the dragon says and gives me a severe look. "We'll wait until you're on your feet and no longer. I must find Phoenix and save her if need be."

"Count me in."

"Excellent. Well, I suppose if you're going to pass the time, you'll be wanting this."

She walks out of the light and returns with a battered copy of *Pride & Prejudice* in her outstretched paw. I shake my head and take it from her.

"And my ebook reader?" I ask.

"Didn't survive the crash, I'm afraid. Nor your regular clothes. Your Spartan attire, however, is as sturdy as advertised." In her other paw she pulls up a duffle that she drops at my side. "I'm sure it'll be needed in the days to come."

I stare glumly into my lap, smoothing a hand over the ripped and bent cover of Melody's loaner book. "I got that reader for my birthday. My library copy of *Harry Potter and the Half-Blood Prince* is going to expire soon. I'll have no idea how the book ends."

"I could spoil it for you but that would make me a terrible librarian."

My head snaps up—and sets off a string of nerve endings. Ouch. That hurt.

"You're a librarian?"

"Yes, for centuries now. I take it you're an avid reader, despite the fact you haven't read the Harry Potter series until now."

I shrug. "I've been busy."

"Pursuing Jane Austen."

"*Commanded*, more like."

"And what writing would you prefer apart from J.K. Rowling? Ernest Hemingway, perhaps?"

"No thanks. Arthur Conan Doyle. Agatha Christie."

"James Patterson?"

"When the mood hits me."

"Brandon Sanderson?"

"Very interesting. Prolific too."

"J.R.R. Tolkien?"

"Absolutely."

She makes a sound almost like a cat purring. "I should have told you I was a librarian from the beginning. I would have earned your trust much faster."

I don my best poker face to hide my delight. "Possibly."

The dragon stretches her neck towards the ceiling and sends a shake down her body, setting her spine spikes swaying. "I must check the perimeter once again and get you something to eat. The sooner you recover, the better."

She stalks out into the darkness. After a few seconds, the light in the room changes so I'm not under an interrogation bulb. The center light dims and the rest evens out so I can see the rest of the room. I take it she knows how my abilities work with line of sight. Trust goes both ways it seems.

With Scholar gone, my eyes fall back to *Pride & Prejudice* in my hands.

I had been in a drug-induced delirium in the hospital when Phoenix read part of it to me. I woke up to her talking about love and pride and understanding her true feelings. I thought for a moment . . .

But no. She was reading a book. Those words weren't hers. They weren't meant for me.

Yet, for a moment I thought they were.

My grip tightens on the book in my hands.

Wherever Phoenix is, whatever trouble she's in, I'll find her.

The Past

I'm in the middle of soaring over the Rocky Mountains with a host of gryphons at my back and the wind in my face when my social worker walks in.

"Charlie."

I keep my eyes pinned to the pages of the book trying to recapture the moment of flying amongst an army ready to fend off evil but she clears her throat, refusing to be ignored. That magnificent world shatters apart, sending me crashing back to reality where I'm seated at a table in the middle of the gryphons' library. She takes the seat across from me and smiles. The same stupid smile she gives me every time.

"How are you doing today, Charlie?" she says and clasps her hands together on top of the table.

"I'm reading right now."

"That's good. So you're enjoying the library?"

She doesn't understand that I want to *keep* reading and not talk to her.

"I wouldn't be here reading if I didn't."

"Hmm, that's true." She pulls out a folder from her brief-case and lays it beside her hands. "Did you do the assignment I asked you to?"

I lower my eyes to the worn pages of the book and aimlessly run my fingers up and down the tooth of the paper. Miss Forland asked me to make a list of things I'm thankful for and things I like. The only thing I've put on it is "books." There's nothing to be thankful for. I don't have friends. I don't care to draw. I don't enjoy sports or anything. I don't really *like* anything I can think of. Except books. All I want to do day in and day out is escape into stories. While lost in someone else's adventures, I don't have to think about my own life.

"Charlie?" she prompts. "Did you write anything down?"

"No."

"Why not? Do you want help with it?"

I hold up a hand to stop her incessant talking. "Miss Forland, leave me alone."

She clicks her tongue. "I just want you to talk to me. And, please, call me Nicole."

"Why?"

Her smile brightens. "Because I want to be your friend. Wouldn't it feel it a bit odd calling your friend by their last name? Charlie?"

I give her a cold look. "Call me Jaeger."

A part of me scolds myself for being so rude. But I don't care. Not really.

"You don't want to be friends?" she asks quietly.

"You're not my friend." I pull the book closer towards me and prop up the side of my face with my hand, angling myself away from her. "That's not why you're here."

No, she doesn't come here by choice. It's been a year since my uncle went out on a mission for the IMS and hasn't come back. He's dead. No one's said it but I know it. People don't just vanish like that unless they're dead. Like my parents. My hands clenches around one of the pages and I nearly rip it. They always leave me behind. Did they even care that I'd be left alone? Did they ever care about me at all?

So Miss Forland comes to check up on me. She makes sure I have a place to stay, that I'm getting food at the cafeteria, and I'm being educated. Kids aren't supposed to be on their own. But she's not my friend. No, I overheard a couple agents talking to Bakari about me. I'm "a difficult case." Not a friend. According to her, I'm cold, melodramatic, have interpersonal issues—whatever that means—and prefer to be isolated. It's not that I like being alone. I would just rather be reading books than pretending to care about other people. None of them actually care about me so why should I do them any favors? Why make friends if they're just going to hurt me in the end? It's stupid. *They* are stupid.

And Miss Forland is really annoying.

She clenches her jaw and shuffles the paperwork in her hands. "I was hoping we'd moved past this by now."

"Past what?"

"Your attitude," she snaps.

I thought her job is to be nice and supportive. She's not even trying now. No one keeps trying for long. They eventually leave me alone but not Miss Forland. She can't. I'm an assignment.

"Let's just go through the checklist." She sighs and pulls out a pen with a firm click on the end. She jots down a few notes without even asking me anything but mutters under her breath, "Has been eating at the cafeteria? Check. Continues coursework? Check. Social interactions?" She doesn't mark anything but looks to me. "Anything magical happen to you yet? Any sign of abilities?"

My face burns and I don't meet her stern gaze.

Draco promised me powers but I haven't shown "an ounce of promise." I heard one of the gryphons say that behind my back. There are a few other Blessed children in the city, two even younger than me. They've already been showing off with what they can do. A scrawny little boy flies around like a stupid buzzing insect all the time. A girl with a unibrow likes to make her drawings come to life. Then there's the bully, Nathan, who can make clones of himself so he can travel as a whole gang of jerks. I do my best to avoid him but it's not too hard. I don't know if he's ever spent more than ten seconds in a library. Or stepped in one. Can he even read?

But me? Nothing. It's been three years since I received the three silver marks on my arm. I'm useless. What was the point of giving me magic if it wasn't going to do anything?

"Nothing strange at all?" Miss Forland persists.

The strangest thing that's been happening to me is sleep walking. I'll go to bed at night, have my usual nightmare about my mother and father dying, and wake up on the other side of the room or out in the hallway. Pretty sure that's not magical though.

I shake my head. There's no way I'm going to talk to *her* about my nightmares. Not that I want to talk to anyone about them. I haven't told a soul that each night I see my parents die. Each time I'm running towards them but can never reach them in time to stop it. I cross my arms over top the open book and tuck my chin into them.

"Are we done?" I ask in a dead tone.

She nods but says, "Please try to do that assignment. It'll help. And smile."

The *nerve*. "*Why* would I smile? What exactly is there to smile about?"

"Just smile, Charlie."

"Bite me."

"*Charlie!*"

I leap out of my chair and rush out of the library.

Then nearly collided with General Bakari standing just outside the doorway—as if he's been there the entire time. Face burning, I hesitate for only a second before breaking into a full sprint down the hallway away from the library and Miss Forland. I keep on running until I reach the edge of the great Pit. I slow to a halt and watch as a squadron of gryphons swoops up out of the hole in a wing formation. The air of their passing pushes me back a step. I watch a moment longer as they round gracefully in the air to speed back the way they came. After a glance back towards the library, I take the narrow steps up between the levels of the aerie and slip between gryphon roosts to a little cubby of stone up high where I have the best view of the gryphons training.

The gryphons don't really let anyone up here so I have to be stealthy. I've been kicked out a few times but others have simply clicked their beaks and let me stay. I'm not in anyone's way here so I guess they don't mind as much.

The squad flies up again and around and between the massive pillars that reach all the way to the ceiling far above. Each turn is graceful and effortless. I wonder what it would be like to be up there with them riding on one of their backs. But of course I can't. No one rides a gryphon. Only a few people ever have. I read about it in *Golden Tails: The Brave*. It detailed the story of a man the gryphons called "Strongheart." He was a hero who saved one of their aeries from a wildfire. He just about died doing it too. When the fire rose and he was the last one left, unable to flee, the gryphon general ferried him away from the danger. I've read that book about four times now.

I wrap my arms around my legs and sigh. I wish I had brought my book with me when I fled the library. I was right in the middle of a really good part. The gryphons were about to save a city in Egypt from a monster occupation during the last great war. The scene of it fills my mind as my eyes follow the gryphons in the air before me—as if they're flying into that battle. Like I'm a weary traveller on the road waiting for rescue when I spot them. I'd run after them into the midst of the action and save them from dangerous arrows. Maybe they'd even call me Strongheart.

The fantasy playing out in my head is interrupted by an odd squeak. I search in the direction of the noise and spot a gryphlet near the lower edge of the aerie watching the flying gryphons with the same awe as me. It's a tiny little thing with awkward feathery tufts and paws far too large to fit its rear legs. Gryphlets aren't cute. They're ungainly and look misshapen until they grow up. This one must have escaped from the protected hatcheries where the young are raised.

I watch as the gryphlet walks on stiff legs with an odd gait towards the lip of the aerie edge. It must be pretty young or a newly hatched gryphlet. It's moving like it's drunk. The squad of gryphons wing fast and furious towards the ceiling at a near ninety degree angle. I crane my neck up to see. The gryphlet does the same.

That's when I spot it tumble forward out of the corner of my eye.

The pitiful thing lets out an earsplitting SQUAWK as it falls right over the edge, bumps off the lower ledge and rolls for the pit.

I'm the only one paying attention. There are no other gryphons close enough to grab it. If no one does anything, it's going to plunge to its death right before me.

Not again.

My body moves of its own accord. I lurch forward as if I was mere feet away to catch it even though I'm halfway across the aerie.

But then I'm not.

Suddenly I'm right where I wish I could be. My toes catch the top edge of the pit as I dive forward to grab the gryphlet before it plunges into the darkness. I grasp its back leg. Victory!

My toes slip right off the ground.

Then we're both falling into darkness.

My cries of panic mix with the screeches of the gryphlet. There's nothing but air and darkness beneath us. I try clumsily to grab the rock wall nearby but only manage to rip off the ends of my fingernails and leave bloody smears behind on the unforgiving stone. The gryphlet tries to flap its wings but it's useless.

We roll over and over again in the air. I keep a grip on its leg and tuck it in to my chest to wrap my arms around it, curling my body into a protective ball.

When we hit the bottom, maybe the gryphlet will be able to survive. Maybe I'll have made some sort of difference.

A boom of wings comes from below. The wind rushes past me as a golden shape races up to meet us. The gryphlet lets out a sharp cry as it also notices the adult gryphon flying to our rescue from the bottom of the pit. The gryphlet's sharp claws dig into my arms and I flinch, almost letting go of it.

Our rescuer maneuvers for us but everything is happening so fast. He soars up with talons outstretched. We meet in a midair collision and one of his talons scraps along my back as he tries to hook my shirt. His other thrusts towards my interlocked arms to grab hold of the gryphlet.

There's a loud sound of fabric ripping and blinding pain.

The gryphlet is safely pulled out of my arms but I continue to fall into the abyss.

I can't breathe. Out of the darkness black water rises to meet me.

Maybe I won't feel anything at all. Maybe it'll be just like falling asleep. I'll slip into that water and simply disappear.

Or maybe I'll feel it as every bone in my body is crushed and I'm flattened like a pancake.

The terror of it—realizing I don't want to die—wakes me up.

I twist my body about in the air so I'm not facing that watery death and instead look to the air above where the gryphon is trying to dive to meet me first. That gryphon can save me. I only need to—

I'm buffeted by downy feathers as I'm suddenly at the gryphon's side with my arms circled around its neck. It gives a throaty caw and hastily stops its plunge towards the bottom. Massive wings beat in powerful strokes on either side, each motion threatening to loosen my death grip. We finally stop falling down and start rising up. My head spins as I can still hardly draw breath. The Pit is endless but with each flap of the gryphon's wings, we rise a little higher. The gryphlet clutched in the oversized talons is wide-eyed and trembling.

After what feels like hours—my arms shaking and burning from holding on so tightly—we finally reach the top of the Pit and open commons of Dreamland. The gryphon lands awkwardly on the ground and I immediately drop onto the hard stone. A crowd swarms us made of anxious gryphons and IMS agents wondering what on earth happened. I roll onto my side and remain that way while I suck down air. The gryphlet is nuzzled by what must be its mother and scooped up into gentle talons.

"Keshiana," she murmurs to her baby.

It's alive. Not that I did much of anything to help, not really. I just managed to get myself in the same predicament.

My heart pounds and with each beat the pain throughout my body becomes sharper. I grimace and shaking takes over me. Panic tightens my throat when I take in my bloody fingers, the red splotches all over myself, and the terrible pain down my back from where the gryphon missed its grab for me.

Hands are suddenly on me, voices telling me to stay calm, that they'll help me. Other voices join in growing louder, demanding an explanation. Some ask if I tossed the gryphlet into the Pit. I can't manage a single word to tell them what really happened. In the midst of the rising clamor, the little gryphon leaps out of its mother's grasp to scramble towards me. It pushes its head between the arms and legs of the IMS agents crowded about to nudge me with its tiny beak and coos faintly as if worried.

I realize I'm crying.

The yells quiet and the talk becomes muffled.

One of the agents scoops me up into their arms and carries me away from the chaos at the edge of the pit. I'm brought to the infirmary where the stone walls and carvings are replaced with green plaster and crisp, clean air. A couple of nurses and a doctor quickly come over to inspect me as I'm set on a white bed and told once again that everything is going to be okay.

More than ever, I wish there was someone here to hold my hand like family. Someone I could trust and know they aren't just assuring me because they have to. That little grpyhlet, Keshiana, immediately had a mother at her side to comfort her. All the gryphons wanted to make sure that little one was safe and unharmed. No one would have cared if I didn't come back out of the Pit.

There's no stopping the sobs that rip out of my chest.

The nurses continue their work as I cry and rage at them every time they make the hurts feel worse. Eventually a guard comes in to hold me while they clean my fingertips and stitch the gash down my back. When they finally finish, my hands and torso are completely covered in bandages. I'm confined to a small room with a fake window overlooking a field of flowers. I'm told not to leave but the door is left open so a nurse can keep an eye on me from her station outside.

The sobs have finally stopped but now everything is dead

inside. I sit upright on the bed, hands held uselessly in my lap, and remain motionless. My eyelids are heavy and my body limp.

Part of me wishes that gryphon hadn't saved me, that I hadn't somehow *leapt* to it. I should have kept falling.

A shadow looms in the doorway and I look up to find General Bakari there. He has to tuck his wings in tight to his sides to enter the room.

"Charlie."

He sits on his haunches at my bedside. I can't bear to look at him.

"I know what happened," he says.

I keep my eyes on my bandaged hands.

"The magic in your blood has finally made itself apparent. You did well."

There are no more tears left to cry but the pain in my chest grows heavier.

"I didn't do anything," I mutter.

"You have developed a rare talent, one that few in history have possessed. The ability to teleport." My dead eyes lift to him. "To be able to move simultaneously through space and time from one location to another." His chest puffs up a bit. "It sparked in your blood to save an innocent life in danger. Your heart is pure, dear boy."

"I don't care."

"The truth, I believe, is that you care very much."

"It doesn't matter. None of it matters." The words start pouring out before I can stop them. "I'm *useless*. I'm stupid. No one would have cared if I didn't come back."

"That's not true."

"*Then why does everyone leave me?*" I thunder. "No one wants me! I don't belong anywhere. I'm just *baggage*."

"Who ever told you such a thing?"

I clench my aching hands and look away. "No one."

"My boy, we all have a purpose. I have told you this before. Your life has meaning. What do you think is more meaningless? Throwing your life away without even trying? Or using it for good?"

"Trying is so hard . . ."

"Things worth having will always take effort. But it *is* worth it."

I want to argue but I don't have the energy to. I'm so tired and wish I could vanish into nothingness. It would be easier.

There's a soft knock on the door. I don't even bother to raise my head. But a few seconds later, there's a scampering sound and a ball of underdeveloped feathers and fur leaps into my lap, startling me.

"Someone wanted to say thank you," Bakari says softly.

The little baby gryphlet I tried to save earlier curls in my wounded hands, its mother watching from the doorway. The pain in my fingers isn't so bad despite it rubbing against the bandages. It rests its beak on my wrist and closes its eyes as if content to remain there forever.

My mind begins to lift out of the darkness suffocating me and I gently lay a hand on its back.

Maybe I could try.

Just a little.

Present Day
Part 4

The wind is knocked out of my lungs when I attempt to teleport from one side of the room to the other. I brace my hands on my knees, breathing hard, and try to ignore the terrible pain in my side. While my scrapes from jumping out of the van have scabbed over and are healing, the bullet wound is taking much longer to overcome. I'm impatient and restless. I wish Scholar could do more to help things along but with magic in my blood, the only thing she can do is the same treatment I'd get from any regular doctor. No speed healing for me. I'm starting to wish that was my special ability right about now.

It's an effort to even out my breathing and stand up straight once more. Well, I can teleport without fainting so that's something. I'm not entirely useless.

Scholar steps through the door in her preferred human

form carrying a tray with hot soup, bread, and her green health concoction.

"That was better," she says and sets the tray on the table beside the hospital bed.

I'm sick of this room, of this little underground hideaway of hers, but it's been too risky to go topside. I do my best to be patient but I keep imagining the trouble Phoenix could be getting into and it keeps me pacing. She can handle herself. I know that. But she does have a tendency of doing reckless things. I can easily see her jumping in front of a bullet or claws for a teammate, running dry of her magic and not being able to defend herself and—

"How much longer do you think we'll be here?" I ask.

"Not long now." She crosses her arms over her chest. "So, what's the theory today?"

I take my time stretching very slowly and carefully. "So we've established you're not a criminal but you're on the run. Draco wants you dead. You don't have any warrants for your arrest with the IMS that you're aware of. However, your house in Sturgeon Lake is still being staked out by IMS agents under misleading orders from Draco. And you're not a patsy for something."

"Well summarized."

"So that means this is personal for Draco." Sweat gathers on my forehead and I feel a little dizzy as I finish my very easy stretches. "A vendetta of some sort. But you're not a criminal so you couldn't have done something illegal against him. It had to have been a different sort of slight. Of pride perhaps? But seeking your death seems extreme for that. So . . . what is worthy of seeking your death?"

"What indeed," she says quietly.

"Death of a loved one. Perhaps you had an unwitting role in it."

She stands stoic without moving a muscle.

"Am I closer this time?" I ask.

"Closer. Much closer."

I consider that for a moment and walk stiffly over to the bed, hiding my pain and doing my best not to grimace. While normally a person's personal matters would be up for guessing, majestic class dragons are the celebrities of the magical side of the world. Their lives have been recorded in great detail. One of the most significant losses recorded for Draco was that of his mate, Nymeria, during the last great war. She died during the conflict at the hands of the werewolves that were fighting alongside Echidna. It was a story that always resonated with me. Draco and I shared something in common—losing someone we loved because of werewolves.

But if Scholar was involved in that, it would mean she was somehow indirectly involved in Nymeria's death. By extension, that would mean she had involvement with the werewolves—with Echidna, the Mother of Monsters.

"You've concluded something," Scholar says. "Something unsavory I assume given your sudden stiffness."

I ponder the wisdom of sharing my theory. If I'm right, then Scholar could reveal her double-sided treachery. She's helped me heal and helped Phoenix before, but there are all sorts of methods of getting what you want from people. Being their friend and associate is an easy way of doing that. But she already knows I'm suspicious of her despite her assurances. She could continue her game and let the situation play out to whatever end she's attempting to achieve. I'm using her at this point as much as she could be using me. She's given me a relatively safe haven to heal away from the threat of the mimics. As soon as I'm well enough, I could easily give her the slip in order to find and rescue my teammates. For the time being, however, since our interests appear to be aligned, I'll continue to play along.

Scholar said before that Phoenix can cure what ails her. From what I understand of Phoenix's abilities, the most powerful thing she's trying to "cure" is the werewolf disease. An ailment for sure. Then if my theory is nearer the mark and she was working with werewolves . . .

Perhaps . . . perhaps this dragon's ailment *is* the werewolf disease. It's a sound theory. There have been reported cases of Blessed being bitten. With their own magic clashing against the werewolf disease in their veins, most go mad or die. The rare case manages to survive but is monitored extremely closely, their life never the same again.

Phoenix was a rare case. More rare than any recorded before. During her confessional, she shared how she had been bitten during her time in Moose Lake. How she overcome the disease. How there were no side affects. She did the impossible.

"So were you bitten before or after your involvement in Nymeria's death?" I ask and hover before the tray of food, my gaze holding steady to the dragon before me.

Her tail twitches. "I think Alona actually underestimated your intelligence."

"So was it before or after? Considering the alpha's ability to control the werewolves, make them do whatever he wants, should I assume you were bitten before Nymeria's death? Perhaps compelled to have some part in it?"

"It was after," she says quietly. Her frill lays flat—like a distressed dog with its ears flat. Her eyes lower to her paw and she watches as she extends and contracts her claws. "Can you imagine having your strength stripped away, to fight to keep what little you have day in and day out for an eternity? Would you not search the world over for a chance of relief from your pain? I have been searching for centuries for someone to end the suffering. Each glimmer of hope in a rising star has ended in disappointment. But Phoenix . . . perhaps after all this time . . ."

I get it. I can understand that drive, the same for many characters in the books I've read seeking salvation and healing, either for themselves or someone else.

"And Nymeria? What happened to her? How did you have a hand in her death?"

She slowly rises on all four paws. "You should eat your food before it gets cold." Then she turns tail and slinks out the door.

Right. She'll answer all my questions and I'm a unicorn. She's made it a guessing game and only plays when she feels inclined to answer.

I keep reminding myself that Phoenix trusts this dragon. At least, the evidence points to that. After spending so much time with Phoenix and the Spartans, I've grown more paranoid and suspicious of everything. The answers to riddles are no longer straightforward and can't be taken at face value.

After devouring the food, my mind sets to work on creating worst case scenarios for my current predicament and the mimics' goals. The same thing I've been doing for the past week.

The same thing I've been doing all my life, really. What if the mimics have already wiped out the leaders of the IMS and taken their places? What if there's no way to identify them until they're trying to kill you? What if they found the team? What if they killed them? What if the mimics *win*?

I release a slow, steady breath as my muscles tense and my abdomen aches horribly. With one hand I apply gentle pressure to the spot and lean over the edge of the bed.

I stretch. I rest. I read. I eat. I repeat.

I get really sick and tired of this crap.

But that's how the day goes, and the one after that, and the one after that, until I've been cooped up for nearly two weeks. I'd go mad if it wasn't for Scholar bringing me books. I burn through Brandon Sanderson's latest, reread a few James Patterson thrillers, and try out a couple from Sarah J. Maas. I let myself drift away into different worlds to forget about my own pain and worries. It's always been this way. Reading is my means of escape and the best form of morphine I have. It numbs the wretched sense of self at least for a little while. I connect with book characters more than real people. In books there's a plan, there's a reason for why people do the things they do, and everything leads to a clearly defined ending. But in real life, people don't make sense, there's no plan or purpose—just chaos.

At least, that's what I've thought for the longest time. I haven't had anyone to ground me in the world, not really. My parents are just ghostly memories. My uncle would be the atypical villain in any book. I don't think I could ever make it as a main protagonist. Maybe a background or third tier character at best. No one wants to read about a grump, a general screwup, and pathetic sob story. No, I don't imagine anyone would care to read about my life.

But John Kessler—he could be the hero of his own story. His group of comrades—Alona, Melody, Theo, and Phoenix—would all be compelling characters.

And Phoenix—she'd be the heroine I'd want to read about, would cheer for to succeed. Would fight for. Would cry over. Would do anything for.

The days pass in stagnant formation until I'm nearly driven insane. I pace and read and chat with Scholar on occasion who no longer feels like playing the guessing game about her past. No, now she's become all about the mission—find Phoenix and save her. It trumps capturing a mimic and finding out its weaknesses.

"But we still need to," she says as she paces in her human form. "That much is obvious."

"We need to rally the IMS," I say from my spot on the bed massaging the sore muscles around my stomach. "Before it's too late."

"I fear it's already too late for them."

"We need the IMS if we're going to fight this war. If they don't know about the threat, they can't counter it. We'll need their help to rescue Phoenix and the team."

"We cannot risk it."

"Yes, *I* can."

She levels a frosty frown at me. "You want to separate? And leave yourself vulnerable?"

"You don't need me."

"On the contrary, your ability makes you exceptional."

"I'm not a tool to be used," I growl.

"We're all tools to be used," she says under her breath and continues to pace. "But perhaps this is a task we cannot achieve alone. I do not trust the IMS but . . . perhaps there is another group we can go to for aid."

"I take it you have someone in mind?"

She pauses, eyes filled with deep thoughts. "I believe you are familiar with the gryphon armada stationed in Dreamland."

Dreamland. I sigh and shake my head. "You don't trust the IMS, but you want me to go talk to their military force? What's the difference?"

"Gryphons are resilient to most types of magic and very good at sniffing out enemies. I would not be surprised if the mimics have stayed far away from Dreamland because of them. If you were to go inform any part of the IMS about the existence of the mimics, it should be them. The gryphons and I may not see eye to eye on many issues, but in this task they can be relied upon. We need them."

"Well, by that logic, why shouldn't I just go tell a centaur? Or a faun? Or something else non-human that we don't think mimics can turn into?"

"Because all others reside in small forces no matter where you find them. While the centaurs may be able to help us, I think you would have a harder time convincing them. The gryphons, however, are concentrated in Dreamland. And their general knows you. You should be viewed as a reliable source. Once you are inside their protection, you will be better guarded than with any other faction. They have the most pull in the IMS apart from the dragons."

I clamp a hand to my forehead and squeeze my eyes shut. "Okay, let's say I make it to Dreamland in one piece. What are *you* going to do?"

"It's time I go to France to find out what I can about our missing Spartans. You'll be safe as you can be with the gryphons. I'll see you to their doorstep but then I must leave. We've wasted too much time already."

My eyes narrow. "Why the sudden change now?"

She clasps her hands behind her back and stands rigid. "While you've been recovering, I've been doing what I can to glean information from a nearby IMS post."

I sit up straighter. "And?"

"A report has been circulated that Team Sierra turned traitor in France and aided in the efforts of Dasc's assaults. They're to be court-martialed. You included."

My entire body slumps and I stare at the far wall. They've made us traitors. It was bad enough when they wanted to kill us. Now they want to smear our names, make us not even worth listening to if we manage to make it to anyone who would have the power to do something about the mimics.

"Why didn't you just say that when I suggested involving the IMS?" I snap. "And you still want me to go Dreamland?"

"I was getting to that."

"Maybe you shouldn't be so long winded then and just get to the point."

Her eyes briefly turn to angry slit eyes before morphing back into their human shape.

"Rude," she says and hisses.

"Pretending to care takes too much energy."

She makes a distinctive growling sound before saying, "It's a risk, but I think it will be worth it in the end."

"If I can make it to them without getting caught and if they don't just hand me over on the spot."

"You were the one that insisted on gathering allies, remember? Would you rather take on the mimics by yourself without any aid? Or is the risk of reaching the gryphons not worth the effort needed to save your friends?"

I level a cool look at the dragon. "I'm accepting the risk. I just want the details to be on the table. We're the only ones free that know of the mimics and can help the team. If one of us goes down, the other has to make it somehow. Everything depends on us."

"I suppose it does, doesn't it?" She gives me a rare smile. I don't think I've ever seen her smile, come to think of it. Not during the entire three weeks or so I've been trapped down here. "In that case, we better prepare."

Striding over to her little medical setup, she begins pulling out clean bandages, anti-septic, athletic tape, and various other sundries for the road that I'll need while still recovering. I slide off the bed and gather up my small pile of clothes—my Spartan gear that Scholar recovered and a couple generic pieces she procured for me.

We're in the midst of loading up a couple of duffles when the lights in the room begin blinking red. There's no audible alarm but if the perimeter sensors are tripped—as Scholar has told me—the lights will flash to give us warning. Our eyes connect across the room.

The dragon looks agitated. "Grab the rest and head out the trap door. I'm not taking any risks that this is a false alarm."

I zip up my duffle and sling it over my shoulder, my lower torso protesting at the movement. "What about you?"

"I'm going to take care of whatever's topside." She makes for the door and in between steps she transitions gracefully into her dragon form. "Make a run for it, Charlie. I'll find you after. You'll know me when you see *me*." She gestures a clawed paw to her dragon self, then leaps through the door and pounds up steps to the main entrance of the hideaway.

Dang it. I wanted to plan better. I can handle myself but running on the fly never works as well as thinking things through ahead of time. I jog to the medical cabinet and load a few more bandages into the bag Scholar had been preparing along with pain medication. Skies above, I'm sure I'll be needing some. While I do so, I begin calculating the best routes to Dreamland to evade the IMS and local authorities.

Slinging the bag over my other shoulder, I make for the back of the room when footsteps thunder down the steps. I swivel around the heart monitor cart so it's between me and the door before a figure emerges in the doorway.

It's Scholar in her human form slightly out of breath. When she sees me, she motions for me to follow her. "Charlie, we have to go."

"Who was outside?" I ask.

"An IMS specialist must have tracked me somehow. I took care of him but we have to move. This location's been compromised."

I nod and move partway around the cart as if I intend to follow her.

But this isn't Scholar. During our weeks together, we've made a few things clear. If Scholar tells me to do something, then that's the plan. Coming back after a few moments with completely different instructions is not something she would do. In her human form no less.

"Okay, hold on," I say and dig into the medicine cabinet alongside the heart rate monitor.

"Come on!"

"Yeah, but we need this. Catch."

I toss a roll of white bandages towards her. Surprised, she fumbles to grab what I've thrown to her. In the same moment, I teleport to her side and stab a surgeon's scalpel into her neck while she's distracted.

"You're not Scholar," I say quietly as she gurgles blood and collapses to the floor.

There's no time to wait around to see if more imposters make it in—or to see what's happened to Scholar. Slightly out of breath, I jog to the back of the room, shove aside the rolling tray against the wall, and wrench open the trap door that blends seamlessly into the tile. I chuck both bags down the dark void and start to climb down the metal ladder attached to the inside of the tunnel.

A pair of hands appear to shove me off the ladder. I catch a fleeting glimpse of Scholar's distorted human face, the side of her neck bleeding profusely, before I'm tumbling down. I fall at an awkward angle, slam sideways against the wall with my shoulder, and whack the side of my head on the cement before one foot hooks on the ladder and twists my ankle painfully. I reach out blindly and manage to grab a rung at the same time I land on my hip, both legs at odd angles. I crumple on top of the two bags I had dropped down and pain reverberates through every part of me.

I can't draw in a proper breath but manage to roll away from the tunnel opening above in case the imposter—a mimic to be sure—starts shooting or throws that scalpel down after me. I'm left blind in the darkness, one hand snagging in the straps of a duffle as the clunks of footsteps travel down the metal ladder. I can try running but it won't do me much good with this mimic chasing after me. I need to get out of here and make it to the gryphons who seem like my last hope now. And are so very far away.

I shuffle down the tunnel pressing one hand to my side with the other hauling along which ever duffle I managed to snag. I go a few steps in the pitch black before stopping and squatting low to the floor.

The mimic's soft laughter echoes off the walls. I can't teleport in this blanket of darkness, unable to see. It must think it has me trapped. That's a mistake on its part. Ever since I developed my ability, I've known my weakness has been not being able to see. It became even more evident when I foolishly got captured by the lamia a couple years ago. That's why I've trained to make sure I'm not vulnerable even when blind.

My senses sharpen as I draw in my breath, not moving a muscle, and focus on the sound of the mimic's soft footsteps drawing closer. At the precise moment when the mimic must sense where I am as well, I strike. An elbow into the mimic's gut followed by a fast jab upwards into its chin to knock it back. The edge of the scalpel nicks the length of my forearm. *There.* I snag the mimic's arm and twist it round until the hand gripping the scalpel can no longer hold it. With it's weapon gone, the struggle in the dark becomes a brutal twisting and bashing of limbs. I get the breath knocked out of me several times when the monster's attacks hit the healing wound in my abdomen. I'm laid out after one such lucky hit and fall backwards onto the floor. My scrambling fingers touch metal and I grasp the fallen scalpel just as the mimic dives for me.

Metal blade meets flesh over and over again until the mimic's attacks slow. I shove it off of me and feel for its neck in the inky blackness of the tunnel. Not letting myself think, I strike again and again until the mimic no longer moves. Warm, sticky blood covers my hands. I fall against the side of the low tunnel and hyperventilate, unable to take a full breath with the pain wrenching my insides.

Thumps sound from the tunnel entrance above. I need to keep moving. I grab the duffle beside me and limp down the tunnel towards the exit, my twisted ankle smarting. My head spins so I brace one hand on the side of the tunnel to keep me steady.

Keep going. People are counting on you. Just keep putting one foot in front of the other.

It gets harder with each step. Warmth trickles between my fingers and down my side. My wound must have reopened.

If you stop now, you're pathetic. You've had worse. Stopping now means giving up. Don't be the person your uncle thinks you are. Don't be a failure. Don't be such a wimp.

The tunnel stretches on forever. I'm disoriented without any light to show me the way. At least I don't hear footsteps behind me. Maybe Scholar managed to stop them. Maybe she got captured and they decided not to go after me. I'm probably not worth as much as the dragon if my suspicions are correct.

My feet catch as the tunnel begins to rise. It's agonizing pushing myself on. But I do. I keep going until I almost run face first until the end of the tunnel and another metal ladder that leads out. Groaning, I haul the duffle over my shoulders and grasp a cold, slick rung. Hauling myself up is no easy task. People recovering from gunshot wounds are not meant to be fighting monsters, walking miles, and climbing ladders. I doubt that would be prescribed physical therapy.

My arms are shaking so much that it's difficult to open the grate above my head. I pull myself out of the tunnel, drop the duffle on the ground, and fall down next to it while I try to catch my breath.

What a pain.

I blink against the faint light coming in through a window and bring the room around me into focus. It's a small, disused, and filthy little hut. A cold wind howls through the wooden planks that make up this little "cabin" of Scholar's. I'm somewhere near the St. Louis River. That's about as much as I ever knew of where Scholar's hideaway was. Finding my way to transportation was always going to be something I figured out myself. The only clue Scholar told me ahead of time was to head north if I ever used this entrance. *Find the trail and keep walking.*

Big help that dragon is.

Easing myself into a sitting position, I close the trap door and bar it with a couple of old locks left lying on the floor amidst leafy debris. Shivering, I turn to the duffle and discover it's my Spartan gear. The medical supplies got left behind. Looks like I'm going to need to improvise. Well, it's no good trying to fix myself up with the blood on my hands from a mimic. That's just a disaster waiting to happen.

Instead, I pick myself up, bleeding side and all, grab the duffle, and open the creaky splintered door.

I'm surrounded by towering birches and pines, shaggy underbrush, slick stones jutting out of the earth, and the smell of decaying leaves courtesy of autumn. I sway on the spot as I orient myself to my surroundings. The rush of the St. Louis River is heard loud and clear to my left. Faint moonlight paints the world with a blend of grays but glistens bright off the jagged, wet stones in the direction I hear rushing water. That way then.

Picking my way carefully through the underbrush and grasping the rough bark of trees to keep upright, I make my way towards the sound of the river. It's an arduous task and I slip more times than I'd like to admit before I break through the trees and stand on a rocky outcropping overlooking the raging froth and foam of the St. Louis River. It curves through and splits the forest, a mighty force to behold. Looking northward up it's length, I see a familiar bridge over it in the far distance, it's stony pillars glinting in the moonlight. The swinging bridge. So that's where I am. Jay Cooke State Park.

I've come here a couple times before when helping Melody check up on a family of fairies that live in the park and kept causing mischief during trail marathons.

With a sigh, I navigate the treacherous footing to the edge of the river and kneel to wash my hands in the turbulent water. It's freezing and with the cold wind, my teeth start to chatter. Pulling out my plain clothes, I use them to scrub the blood away and towel off quickly. I take my time doing it right, although I keep tossing glances over my shoulder in the direction of Scholar's little hideaway. How she's managed to keep it hidden in the middle of Jay Cooke without being discovered, I have no idea. Maybe she's friends with a park ranger.

Once properly cleaned off, I strip out of my wet and filthy clothes. It's a struggle to get into my Spartan gear but I manage somehow. Although I'm still floating in a world of pain, I feel better in the protective suit. After making sure I have all of the important things out of the duffle, I stuff most of the dirty clothes into it and chuck the bag into the river. It's quickly dragged away by the current out of sight. With only my filthy shirt left, I rip off a chunk, catch it on a stick wedged between the rocks, and leave it there to be found by any pursuers. Hopefully, they'll take time to search the river thinking I stumbled in. Once satisfied with my false trail, I focus on a point near the bridge that's lit just enough by the moonlight to see, and port away.

And nearly fall over when I reach my intended destination. I catch myself on a tree and take shaky breaths.

I never want to be shot again in my life.

No time to pity myself though. There's only the mission.

I push ahead through the trees, startling up deer and the like on my way to the bridge. It's with relief that I reach the end—until I realize the other end is completely destroyed. I forgot about that. The floods earlier in the year caused a heck of a lot of damage in the area, this bridge included. My face falls flat. Scholar knew about this. Figures. I tramp across what remains of the bridge and go as far as I can. Remnants of the other side, broken beams and posts, still remain hanging partway into the waters below. Setting my sights past the wreckage, I have to really squint to find a clear landing. After a rough teleport, I fall back against the side of the visitor's center for the park breathing heavily.

I allow a few moments to pass before I pull myself along the side of the building and find a window. There's enough moonlight that I'm able to get through the glass directly to the other side.

Where I crumple into a rack of tourist sweaters with a noisy crash but am luckily cushioned by a bin of stuffed bears and moose. People buy this crap? I kick a stuffed duck away from me and push myself back up. Moving slowly—out of capability rather than want—I browse through the tourist stuff and find a hoodie that fits me to tug on over my Spartan gear. I'd be a little suspicious wandering around in attire that's obviously military. No pants of any kind though to throw over mine. I'll just have to make do.

The world spins in a hazy cloud and I realize I haven't got much time left. Staggering towards what looks like an office, my vision starts to ghost. I shrug through the partly open door into a cramped little space that serves as a sort of janitorial closet. Closing the door behind me, I have just enough time to jam the knob with the end of a broom before I tip backwards and collapse from shock.

The Past

My legs dangle over the ledge of the aerie shelf as I read the fascinating tale of Sir Robert the Red, a knight during the times of King Arthur. Every now and then I look up to watch the gryphons practicing their maneuvers. Next to me is a spread of textbooks and homework assignments that I'm currently neglecting. I'll get around to it at some point, but Sir Robert just encountered a kelpie and is attempting to wrangle it with a magical halter he got from his selkie lover. Besides, Keshiana is taking a nap on top of my Latin notes and I'd rather not disturb her. Her feathers have come in with a stately golden sheen and she's about doubled in size during the past month since our fall into the Pit. Whenever I come to study in the aerie or library, she almost always finds me. She still doesn't speak much yet—although she's nailed "fish" and "no" already. Most of the time she quietly coos and nuzzles my arm with her beak.

She's the best kind of company. Quiet, comfortable, and nonjudgmental.

Ms. Forland has tried to get me to interact with some of the other Blessed children in Dreamland again but I haven't made friends with any of them. I decided books were much more interesting and went back to the library. At least they don't talk back, bully, or do stupid things. There's meaning and purpose to books from beginning to end. But people . . . they're messy and don't make sense half the time. It's annoying.

And yet . . . I wish there was someone I could talk to. Someone that isn't Ms. Forland. I'd hate to bug the general. Plus, he's a bit intimidating.

Sighing, I return to my book and Sir Robert.

Moments later there's a commotion in the distance near IMS headquarters. Keshiana even cracks open an eyelid. I close my book and lean forward a bit to get a better view. A crowd of agents has gathered outside the entrance doors. Applause echoes out to me from across the Pit. What's going on?

"Stay here," I tell Keshiana and set my book down beside her. She blinks in response.

I turn my eyes towards the crowd, to the edge at the rear, and *will* myself to be there. Nothing happens. With a growl, I focus and picture myself standing on the edge of that crowd.

I reappear where I want to. It's taking time to train my abilities. Sometimes it just doesn't want to work. I push through the agents, centaurs, fauns, elves, and even a couple of gryphons also here to see what's going on. Where I can't pass, I teleport to the next spot I can see until I'm at the center.

Director Dunham sees me first. She stands at the center of

attention talking with a man whose back is to me. Her eyebrows lift and she gestures to me, saying something quietly to the man everyone has gathered around. He looks over his shoulder and our eyes meet.

Uncle Laurence. He's alive. After so long and he's . . . he's here. He's alive.

I'm not alone anymore.

He glances at the crowd and his face melts into a smile. "Come here, kid."

I take a nervous step forward but then he turns fully about and opens his arms to me. I stumble forward and fall into his embrace. He pats my back and ruffles my hair. I clutch tightly onto his shirt and squeeze my eyes shut tight. He's never given me a hug, as if accepting me fully. Did something happen during his time away? Did he miss me? But what even happened? What kept him away? Why did it take so long for him to come back?

"It's okay, CJ," he says quietly and rests a hand on top of my head. "Chin up. You're fine."

I lean my head back so I can see him but keep his shirt balled in my fists. "Where were you? What—I thought you were—"

His smile fades and people whisper around us. I can't help the tears that begin to fall. I've been so alone. Maybe this time . . . maybe things can be better. Maybe we can be family.

Bending down on one knee so we're eye level, he says, "How about you wait back at the apartment? I have to talk with the director. Then we'll get some ice cream. Okay, buddy?"

I nod but don't let go of my grip. He has to pry my hands off his shirt before he can stand again. The crowd is silent as he walks with the director into IMS headquarters, leaving me behind. Eventually everyone walks away but I remain where I am staring at the door to headquarters. Something heavy falls in the pit of my stomach. Ever so slowly, I turn around and walk to the apartment where I've been living alone this past year. My feet drag across the reddish stone floors, up the spiral staircase to the second level of apartments, and down the hall to the last door. With a trembling hand I unlock it and slip inside.

Like flipping a switch, the world of magic disappears into a simple home with carpet, beige walls, and gray furniture. You'd never know there was a fleet of gryphons and magic out there if not for the window on the opposite side of the living room overlooking the Pit. It's to that view I'm drawn. I stand at the window and stare out as I hug my arms to myself. My grandfather's bracelet presses into my skin, leaving an imprint of the Latin etched on it. With the assortment of books available, I've been able to translate it myself. It says "for those I love I will sacrifice." I think about it a lot when there's not a book nearby and the memories of those terrible nights in the mountains come back to me. It's something a hero from the books I read would say. There's always someone they're fighting for, either to save or protect. I want that. I want it so badly. Someone to fight for, someone to love. That's part of what family is, isn't it?

I don't know how long I wait at the window until there's a firm knock at the door. Uncle Laurence must be done talking with the director. I'm nervous and have so many questions about where he's been. I find I can't move until there's another knock, louder this time. Nearly tripping across the carpet, I hurry to open the door.

But it's not my uncle in the doorway. General Bakari stands outside filling up the hallway. He's so big that his wings touch the walls on either side.

"General?"

He reaches a taloned foot back to grab something held in his wing, and pulls out the books I left at the aerie with Keshiana.

"You forgot something."

My face burns and I quickly take the books from him. "Oh. I—I'm sorry, general. It won't happen again."

He blinks slowly. "I'm not angry, child."

"Oh." I don't know what else to say and linger awkwardly in the doorway.

"How is your training coming along?" he asks.

I swallow and bob my head. "Okay, I think."

"More than that, I suspect. I hear your testing scores have been excellent. Well done."

My eyes grow wide. He knows about my testing scores? Is he that curious about the random kid always in his aerie? Or does he . . . could he . . .

It's hard to tell with his beak, but it almost looks like he's smiling. "Take care, my boy."

He shuffles as gracefully as he can back down the hallway, his feathers dusting off the walls on his exit. I stand shocked in the open door. Warmth spreads through my chest and I puff up a bit. The general thinks I've been doing well. He thinks my scores are excellent. He *noticed*. The mighty general who's always so busy taking care of his soldiers and the other gryphons. He bothered to care.

I drop the books off on the couch and rush back to the open

window to watch the general exit the apartments. He doesn't leave immediately, though. He paces a bit and fluffs his wings now and then. I wonder what he's doing?

Then he stops and turns about to stand stiffly, the tips of his wings trembling.

My uncle walks up to the apartment but stops before the general who's blocking the way.

Their voices float up to me from below.

"General," my uncle says and sticks his hands in his pockets. "Can I help you?"

"I'd have words with you, boy," the general says. I've never heard him sound so cold and intimidating before.

Uncle Laurence lifts his chin. "*Boy?* No offense, *general*, but this *boy* just foiled a plan years in the making to sic a hydra on this place. So, if you'll excuse me . . ."

General Bakari doesn't move except to extend his wings out farther so there's no way my uncle can pass by. I lean partway out the window watching.

"You are sworn to protect your nephew," the general thunders. "Do you have any idea what that child has been through? He is your ward and you abandoned him for glory."

"Excuse me?"

"True warriors do not forget their charges."

"Was I supposed to just forget about the hydra then?" my uncle says angrily and gestures widely to the city behind him. "Let everyone else die?"

"It is not your responsibility alone to protect this city. And if you had the wisdom to share your intelligence with others, it wouldn't have taken a year for the threat to be neutralized." The general takes a step forward and my uncle leans back. "Charlie is a clever boy who needs his only remaining family to be present, not an absentee fool. And I intend to make sure that boy is looked after."

The general stalks away and buffets Uncle Laurence with a single flap of his wings.

Silence follows and I realize I've stopped breathing. Then my uncle looks up to the window and spots me. I hastily duck back into the apartment as my heart thunders in my ears. Fear grips me. The look on his face is . . . terrifying. I don't know what to do with myself so I simply stand in the middle of the living room holding my hands together tightly and pressed to my chest.

Muffled footsteps echo in the hallway outside before the door opens to Uncle Laurence. He walks quietly inside and shuts the door behind him. There he pauses, eyes glued to the floor before his gaze slowly turns to me.

I swallow.

"What did you say to Bakari?" he asks quietly.

"What?"

He stalks forward and my feet itch to run. "I said, *what did you tell Bakari?*"

"I don't know what you're—"

"Do you have any idea what kind of embarrassment that is?" He towers over me, warm breath in my face, and hands clenched into fists at his sides.

"I—I didn't—"

"I've been out there for months trying to *protect* this city and you go and cry to the gryphon general? What would the director think if she heard that? Huh?" Spit flies and I flinch as it hits my face. "You're a spoiled brat, you know that!"

I can't breathe fast enough and tears well in my eyes. "I didn't—I'm sorry. I—I—"

"Stop stuttering and spit it out!"

My chest heaves and it's difficult to take a full breath. "I didn't say anything!"

"Oh, really?" he snaps. "That's not what I hear from your social worker!" My eyes go even wider. "That's right. I got the full report just now slapped in my face. I protect you, pay for your clothes and food, make sure you have a roof over your head, and you're still ungrateful. I keep putting my life on the line but everyone just wants to talk about you because you won't stop whining! You think you're the only one alone, Charlie? Grow up!"

"Stop it!" I yell and grab at my hair. I can hardly see past the tears now.

"Don't you talk back to me!"

"*Stop it! Shut up!*"

His hand flies out of nowhere and smacks me across the face. The blow is hard enough that I stumble into the couch and the books I abandoned there. Shock steals the air from my lungs and I slowly bring a hand up to my stinging cheek.

He swears loudly, stomps over, and bends down to pull my hand away from my face. I jerk away from him, from the same hand that struck me. He sighs and gives me a stern look. "Look what you made me do, CJ. Stay there. I'll get some ice."

I remain frozen against the couch. My head tells me to run but I don't move. I can't. I don't know what I'm supposed to do. Uncle Laurence returns with a little baggie of ice and holds it out to me.

"Press that against your face."

When I don't move to take the bag, he puts it in my hand and closes my fingers around it. The cold bites into my skin and shakes my senses enough that I hold it lightly against my face.

My uncle slides down against the couch to sit next to me and looses a long sigh.

"Look, kid, I'm sorry. I shouldn't have done that," he says gruffly. "It's been a long year. I've been fighting shapeshifters and trying not to die out there. You don't know what it's been like, CJ. I'm too . . . worked up and I just lashed out. You'll forgive me, won't you?"

My brain's a jumble and I can't form words to respond.

"How about I make it up to you?" he continues. "I'll … buy you some ice cream. Maybe we could watch a movie. That sounds nice, right? We'll spend some family time together. You're all I have too, you know."

I blink away the tears and run the back of my hand under my nose. He keeps his eyes on me, waiting for an answer, so I nod.

"Good." He pats me on the shoulder and gets up. "I have some business to take care of but I'll be right back. Just . . . lay down for a bit. Then we'll go out."

He gives me a smile then walks back out of the apartment.

Several minutes pass before I pull myself fully onto the couch and curl up around the books I dropped there. My Latin notes are crumpled and smell like straw from the aerie. I set the bag of ice down and tuck a pillow over my head to hide like an ostrich in the sand.

Uncle Laurence finds me that way some time later. He pats my back and takes me out to the market to find ice cream. We sit in silence at a table outside the Sweet Emporium and watch the evening supper crowds walk by. Uncle Laurence asks what I've been up to and I answer quietly in short sentences, afraid I'll make him angry again if I say too much or dare to talk about how alone I've been. We spend the rest of the evening walking around—he keeps slinging his arm around my shoulders—and eventually settle in to watch a movie back at the apartment. My uncle tells me it was a favorite of my father's.

When night comes, he wishes me goodnight, turns off the lights, and closes my door softly behind him when he leaves.

I'm still feeling confused when I wake the next morning and enter the living room to find a bag of luggage lying open on the couch. It's mostly full.

"Uncle?" I rub the sleep from my eyes and walk into the kitchen where I find him making an omelet and toast.

"Oh good, you're awake," he says over his shoulder. "Pass me the salt, would you?"

I grab the shaker and hold it out to him. "Are you going somewhere? I saw the suitcase."

"*We* are going somewhere."

"We?"

"Yes, both of us. Take a seat. Are you hungry?"

I nod and sit at the small eat-in counter. He hums as he tosses ham and peppers into the dish and fixes up the omelet. Once done, he puts it on a plate and slides it in front of me.

"Eat up. We'll be leaving in about an hour."

"Where are we going?"

"I'm being transferred to the Midwest for some specialized training. I can't very well leave you here alone, can I?" He grins and brings over two pieces of buttered toast. He's never cooked for me before. "And I think we ought to spend more time together. I can start teaching you what I've learned. Maybe you'll even be able to join me on hunts."

"You want me to hunt monsters with you?"

"We're family, remember? And family sticks together. I'll show you how to be a man. It'll just be you and me, CJ. We're all we have."

He grips my shoulder and gives me a firm shake before walking off into his bedroom.

My earlier confusion lifts only a little. He wants me to stay with him. He wants to be family. An ache so deep goes right through my chest. I don't want to be alone. I want to have what normal kids have. I want a family that wants me just as badly as I want them.

And what happened yesterday . . . I provoked it. Uncle Laurence was just . . .

It won't happen again. I'm sure of it. He's taking me with him. He *wants* me with him.

After eating breakfast, I pack up my own things. Uncle Laurence and I do one last sweep of the apartment to make sure we aren't leaving anything behind before we walk to the lifts. It's then that I realize I don't know if I'll ever come back to this place. I haven't even said goodbye to Keshiana or General Bakari. Will they wonder where I've vanished to? Or will they move on and forget I was ever here?

"On our way out," Uncle Laurence says, "we'll get you some new clothes. You'll need a winter jacket and—"

His eyes narrow on something in the distance and he clenches his jaw. I look ahead to see what's wrong.

General Bakari stands next to the lifts with his emerald eyes on us.

"What's he doing here?" Uncle Laurence says under his breath.

The general meets us partway to the lifts. He and my uncle share a frosty look before the gryphon turns to me.

"I hear you're leaving," he says in a low voice.

"I'm going to the Midwest with my uncle."

"You will be missed, young one."

"I—I'll miss you, too."

He stares at me for a long moment and then leans in to peer more closely. "What's that mark on your face?"

My hand immediately goes to cover my cheek. "What?"

His eyes bore into me. "Is there anything you want to tell me, Charlie? Anything at all?"

"I . . ."

If I told him what happened, I'm not sure what he would do. I'm scared of what he *might* do, though.

I can feel my uncle's stare.

"No."

"You need only say a word," the general says quietly.

"I'm fine. I just fell asleep on a book last night."

My uncle rests a hand on my shoulder. "If you'll excuse us, we have to catch the bus before it leaves. Come on, CJ."

He pulls me away towards the lifts. I look back at the general who watches us with an expression I can't make out—as if he's sad, or maybe angry. I can't tell. But then I'm in the lift with my uncle and we rise up, up, up, and out of the hidden city, leaving the general and gryphons behind.

Present Day
Part 5

I get practice in diversion and escape techniques when I'm woken up the next day by someone trying to force the door open to the closet I've sequestered myself in. Well, I'm awake. Means I'm not dead. All of me is stiff and when I try to move, I find my back sticks to the floor from my tacky and dried blood. Sucking in a sharp breath, I pull up the hoodie and peel back the layer of protective Spartan gear to inspect the damage. The bandage is completely soaked through and there's marked redness stemming from the wound. Lightly pressing a finger to the edge, I also find my skin hot to the touch.

That's not good. I need to get treated quickly before infection spreads.

I'm running on a profound lack of energy so I take my sweet time pulling myself to my feet using the storage racks as pull up bars. Once up, I keep a hand pressed to my side, move the broom aside, and open the door. A tall man in a brown park ranger uniform takes a step back and blinks as I make my exit. It's in that moment of surprise that I grab the ring of keys on his belt. He yells but I swivel until I'm behind him with my hand still on the ring, and then vanish through the window to the parking lot beyond. It's a misty gray morning so I'm quick to disappear from the disoriented ranger. As suspected, I find his park ranger SUV out in the lot. Sorry, pal.

Using the keys I lifted off him, I get into the SUV and gun it out of the lot. One hand remains on the steering wheel but the other is pressed to my side. I need supplies. I need money. I need different transportation because this thing is going to be far too noticeable and will be reported stolen soon enough.

I'll need to be swift, efficient, and avoid surveillance hot spots. Unfortunately, I'm going to have to risk one in order to get the supplies I urgently need. There's not too much IMS agent activity in this area but there's probably more than normal with the hunt for Epsilon still ongoing—and now for me. I think of the sweep Team Sierra and I did looking for signs of Dasc in Bemidji. If the IMS comes to bear down on this area, I'll have very few avenues on which to slip out.

I glance to the brightening sky outside. It's just the cusp of morning still. Businesses will be opening soon. Medical supplies. Pharmaceutical supplies. Hair dye. Makeup. Clothes. Food. Cash. I can't bounce around for what I need. With a sigh, I loop outside the city of Carlton to avoid the jail and Sheriff's office and make for the back roads around the casino nearby that will take me into Cloquet. I keep my eyes open but I'm feeling faint so my level of alertness isn't nearly what I want it to be at. By some miracle, I manage to sneak into the city and make a beeline for the local Walmart. A tingling goes down my spine. It feels foolish to come here—after all, it was at a Walmart where we got our lead during that search in Bemidji. There's plenty of surveillance, but I'm also good at avoiding such things.

I park the vehicle near the front of the lot. It stands out enough that they'll know where I'll have gone. Might as well make this more of a speed trip than sneaky. I pull up the hood of my sweatshirt and keep my head somewhat bowed as I enter the store. It shouldn't be *too* suspicious, not with the chill in the air outside. I note the cameras and hurry inside. Parts of the store have the lights off and are technically closed for the early morning hour of the 24/7 hour store. I take an easy turn to my left and after a quick check of cameras and employees alike, I vanish into the darkened pharmacy area. Keeping low to the counters, and grimacing at the pain the position brings on, I find what I need—a bottle of prescription-strength painkillers and antibiotics—and move out of the area.

The rest I'm quick to scavenge from the store, stuffing things into a reusable bag hanging from a rack. Sure enough, I eventually hear footsteps dogging me. Well, I'm sure someone had to notice me at some point. A bit of quick teleporting leaves my follower in the dust, left confused in the glassed in entrance.

My feet stumble and my breath comes in wheezing pants. I've been using my ability too much and lost too much blood.

Get to the gryphons. That's all that matters. Just get to Dreamland.

Right. Focus.

I stride across the open parking lot and cross paths with a young man rushing to get into the store with a blue employee shirt on. He's in too much of a hurry to avoid me running into him or notice when his keys go missing from his pocket. Hopefully with him going into work, he won't be missing his car for sometime. I know that relying on assumptions is never a good idea though. I keep walking and locate the man's car. Easy.

I rip into the bag of jerky I nabbed from the store as I drive back out of town. I pass a couple of squad cars with their lights on heading in the opposite direction. I keep on without a second glance but that's my time limit now. The distance it takes them to get to the store, find the park ranger's vehicle, scan surveillance footage, and discover the other missing vehicle. Well, this is certainly a pain, especially since I need to stop somewhere to patch myself up before going any further.

So I drive. And I keep on driving—surpassing the point at which I really ought to stop—until I see the exit sign for Barnum in the distance. That'll do. More like, it *has* to do because I can't keep going like this. I pass a gas station, high school, restaurant, and look for a house that doesn't have any cars in the driveway or anyone nearby. No neighbors that might find me parking there to be suspicious. I'm forced to turn down a few short streets before I find the perfect little hideaway. My hands are shaking so much I have trouble gathering up the stuff I stole from Walmart. I walk up the front porch but don't even try the door. There's a good chance it's locked or there could even be a security system. No, I peer through a window that has the curtains drawn back and reappear in the middle of a quaint living room.

Then sway so hard that I collapse onto the sofa.

Yeah, this isn't good.

It's difficult enough for normal people recovering from a

gunshot wound. However, with the additional use of the magic in my blood, it takes an extra toll. I've used it too often, apparently. I thought I could handle more. I grit my teeth against the pain and frustration. I *should* be able to handle more.

Useless. Utterly useless.

You need me, you greasy little runt! Without me, you would've been dead ages ago.

I want to punch something when my uncle's voice comes floating through my head. This always happens. Once I hit that low, every little bad thing in my past comes roaring back to the surface as if the dam has broken. It's always been this way, and it's only been made worse by the fact that I haven't had my antidepressants for some time now—not since my stay at the hospital. I'm surprised I've held out this long, actually. Although, maybe I shouldn't be surprised. Of course, it hasn't been that long. I'm sure other people could do much better.

I close my eyes and focus on relaxing each tense muscle throughout my body.

There's not really a way to stop the thoughts that keep intruding, but acknowledging that I'm going into a spiral helps. Denial has never acted in my favor.

There's a good chance I'm not going to succeed. I'm probably going to bleed out before I even get to the gryphons because I'm a stubborn idiot. Heck, even if I make it to the gryphons, they'll never listen to me. That, or a mimic will finish me off before I can even try.

So why even try?

I press my cold hand to my forehead, wishing I had been smart enough to snag some antidepressants back at that pharmacy and not just pain meds.

Pull it together, Charlie.

Slowly lowering my hand, I stare at my leather bracelet that I managed to retain through the rough exit from Scholar's lair. The metal band gleams with the latin phrase left behind by my grandfather and later passed down to my mother. She ended up gifting it to my father one Christmas. I think it was the only time my parents actually exchanged gifts that meant something. To me, it was like a peace offering to bridge the gap that had come between them. Not that it did much. He was still wearing it when she killed him.

Illis quos amo deserviam.

For those I love I will sacrifice.

Another voice rises to replace my uncle's.

Because we're family. Me, Hawk, Melody, Theo, John, Alona—we're your family. And family looks after one another. We care—heck, we even sympathize—because that's what you do when you love someone. Every single one of us would die for you, Charlie.

That conversation has been etched into my memory from the amount of times I've replayed it in my mind. Phoenix and I were skipping stones at Theo's grandmother's house when neither of us could sleep. The things she said …

She's right though. Team Sierra is family now. The bond goes deeper than service or honor. At least, that's what I'd like to believe. Even now it almost feels as if I'm casting my wants upon the people around me, that the bonds don't actually go as deep as I think. Maybe to them I'm just a coworker. That fear persistently lingers and the doubts of not being good enough always tell me that the ones that show such affection are only doing so out of a need to be polite. It's so hard to think that they might honestly feel that way about me. The seed of doubt is always there.

I slip further down into the spiral, unable to lift myself from the couch of a random stranger's home.

My hand falls limp onto the cushions and my fingers curl as if around an invisible note—one I've now since lost but can still remember each line anyway.

You've become my best friend. I don't want to say goodbye but I have to do this. Promise me you'll always keep fighting, and I'll do the same.

My heart beats a thundering rhythm in my chest.

I have to keep fighting. I have a promise to keep.

It's a struggle to finally pry myself off the couch and make a quick turn about through the house to find what I'm looking for. Moving helps. When I swing into one of the bedrooms decorated with movie posters and a Star Wars bed set, I come to an abrupt halt. A German Shepherd raises its head, stirring out of its nap on the kid-sized bed, its lanky legs hanging over the edge of the mattress that's much too small for it. Neither of us move, eyes glued to each other.

"I don't mean any harm," I say cautiously. The dog's ears twitch. "I just need a few things and I'll be on my way. If you let me pass, I'll get you a treat."

Its ears swivel some more but it remains on the bed, tense and alert.

I give a weary sigh. "You're a good boy, aren't you? Such a good boy."

His tail gives a single thump. I extend a hand slowly and its head lowers as it sniffs me out. After a tense moment, his tongue lolls out and he gives a classic doggo smile. I give him a scratch behind the ears and he doesn't make any move to bite me or growl.

"Such a good boy, but not such a great guard dog, huh?" His tail thumps on the bed. "Let's get you a treat."

I move slowly back out and to the kitchen. The dog follows me and is ever so happy when I feed him a leftover chunk of cold chicken from the fridge. Whatever makes him happy. While giving him a good back rub so he knows I'm a friend, I glimpse the tag on his collar.

"Good boy, Ammo. We're friends. Don't turn on me, please. I don't want to port if I don't have to. I'm so tired, Ammo."

Once he's sated, he follows me around the house as I pick up a few miscellaneous items found while rummaging through the residents' belongings. It feels odd digging through strangers' things and walking past family photos filled with unfamiliar faces. I may not like people but I'm not heartless. I'll have to repay them at some point, even if it takes me a long time.

I eventually peel off my Spartan uniform in the small bathroom with Ammo laying outside the door as a silent sentinel. This family really ought to have a security system. Ammo isn't reliable.

It's a painful and difficult process changing out my filthy bandage, treating the wound, and putting on a clean pad of gauze. While I do so, I leave my Spartan attire to soak in the tub filled with cold water and hydrogen peroxide. It'll be more comfortable to wear once it's free of the dried blood and lingering odors.

Do you still hand wash your shirts in the morning?

I growl to myself and Ammo flicks his ears.

I do my best to focus on the task at hand and push aside

lingering thoughts. I set my mind on cleaning up and changing my appearance. Once the blood is washed from my hands, I raid the fridge. While chowing down on as much reheated lasagna as I can, I change into a plaid shirt and jeans found in the master bedroom and put most of my Spartan gear into the dryer downstairs. Ammo continues to follow me around so I toss him scraps of what I'm eating to keep him satisfied.

Eventually I rest on the couch as I tuck supplies into a backpack I stole from the kid's room. There was also a little nest egg of cash in the nightstand of the master bedroom. It'll tide me over until I get to Dreamland—hopefully.

I fall into a stupor on the couch until the dryer buzzes. After stowing my Spartan gear in with the rest of the food and bandages I've collected, I take one last stop in the bathroom. I've sprayed blue dye into my hair and put heavy eyeliner around my eyes. I'm hardly recognizable as a goth lumberjack now. I just need the ruse to last long enough to get me to the gryphons. Whether it'll be enough or not is yet to be seen.

I walk out ready to leave.

Just as a mother and her young son halt in the hallway by the front door. Our eyes meet and the mother lets out a gasp, dropping the purse from her shoulder. They're bundled up and the boy looks a little ill, as if Mom here just picked up her son from school for being sick. My head whirls.

I hold my hands out before me. "I'm not going to hurt you. This isn't what it looks like."

"*What are you doing here?*" the mother shouts in a shrill voice.

"I'm sorry. I—"

She points a shaking finger at me. "You stay right there!"

Ammo slips around me to head towards his owners but once within a couple feet he pauses. His hackles rise. He takes a slow step backward and begins to growl.

My eyes draw from the dog to the mother and son. Even when I—a complete stranger—entered his house, he never acted like that. It's like he knows there's something wrong. That *they* are wrong.

If there's one thing universally acknowledged in history that neither magic, historians, or experts have been able to explain is that the one species of animal most sensitive to the presence of monsters is dogs. Man's best friend indeed. Man's best sensor when out of other options.

Thankfully I kept my multipurpose monster killing dagger tucked into my belt under the plaid shirt I stole. I shift to wrap my hand around its handle.

"What are you doing?" the woman shrieks and pushes the little boy behind her.

An act a normal mother would do. What if I'm wrong? What if these two aren't mimics or shapeshifters or something else unsavory? What if they're normal and the dog is the one with an issue? What if I attack innocent people?

I walk at an angle towards the couch where my bag of supplies remains.

The boy starts to cry as the mother screams, "Don't move!"

They're certainly convincing if they *are* mimics. I hesitate. Ammo continues to growl and takes one more step backward.

More than ever I wish Phoenix was here. She would know the truth.

And tell me if I'm about to make a terrible mistake.

"What's the dog's name?" I ask and slide the dagger out from its spot in my belt.

The mother glances uneasily at the dog still growling at her, back at her son, turns wide-eyed to me, and draws a gun from the back of her jeans.

In the blink of an eye I'm at the woman's side with my dagger pressed to her throat and wrench the gun out of her hand. Both Ammo and the kid startle, the dog leaping backwards so hard and fast it hits the wall behind it. The kid falls on his butt with a cry and the woman screams.

"What do you want? What are you?" I growl at her ear.

I can feel her trembling beneath my grip.

"I d-don't know what you m-mean," she says and tears slip down her face. "Why are y-you doing this?"

The doubt really begins to settle in. Maybe this *is* just a mother with a permit to carry protecting her child. That still doesn't explain the dog's reaction to these people. But if I'm wrong . . . do I dare take the risk?

"*Please*," she sobs. "I'll give y-you my wallet. Just let my son go."

Sweat beads on my forehead and every muscle in my body is as taut as a bowstring.

Shapeshifters always have small tells. As do werewolves, vampires, and so many other monsters. They can never completely hide what they are. There are no tics here, nothing to mark them as anything more than a little boy and mother coming home to a threatening stranger.

Ammo barks suddenly and I catch movement out of the corner of my eye.

The little boy drives a small fist into my side—right where the worst of my pain throbs. I let out a sharp cry and my body curls up around the shock that goes through me. The woman takes the opportunity to jab her elbow into my ribcage in almost the exact same spot. The breath completely leaves me this time and I fall onto one knee, the dagger knocked out of my hand. When I see a shoe flying up to meet my face, my Spartan instincts kick in from over a year of intense training. I grab the foot and pull hard enough that the woman falls onto her back. Little arms wrap themselves around my neck from behind with surprising strength. Still trying to catch my breath and feeling dizzy, I roll forward to flatten the small body to the floor.

The next several seconds are filled with flailing arms and legs. I manage to extricate myself, aim the gun in my hands and face the mother as she grabs my dagger off the floor. She leans crouched forward with teeth bared while I barely have one knee propped up beneath me. We're mere feet apart. Ammo stands just off to the side barking like mad.

She lunges. The dagger pivots towards my heart.

I fire.

The blast is deafening inside the house.

The woman falls limp to the floor. Blood stains the floor and wall behind her.

Ammo continues to bark like crazy.

Small hands reach for the dropped dagger beside the unmoving body.

I reflexively turn as the boy lunges for me next.

Blackness floods his eyes for a mere second.

So I fire again.

Ringing fills my ears as I lean back against the couch, two

bodies at my feet and blood staining my white socks. The small boy's lifeless face stares up at me, eyes open and pale. The image of his lifeless body is burned into my eyes and I can't look away. Ammo continues to bark wildly beside the carnage.

Ever so slowly, I pull my dagger out of the limp grip of such small fingers. I shakily rise and tug on my shoes in a daze. Utterly numb, it takes me only a moment to find car keys in the purse still sitting on the floor where it was dropped earlier. I grab my bag of supplies and walk to the door. I briefly wonder how quickly a neighbor would have called 911 after those gunshots and the response time of nearby police officers. I stop beside the door to the house, grab a red leash off a hook on the wall, and whistle sharply.

Claws click across the hardwood floor.

"Let's go, boy."

I hook his collar, get into the gray minivan left behind by the people now dead inside the house, make sure Ammo is set-up in the passenger seat beside me, and gun it out of town.

The dog whines now and then as I drive in silence. Unnerved isn't an adequate word for my current state of mind. I try not to think of that little boy's face. It was a mimic. I saw the black eyes just like those agents that tried to kidnap me earlier.

Not a boy. A monster. It was. It had to be.

I drive and drive until I reach a national bus station. Ammo does well on the leash as I pay for a ticket and the driver makes an exception for me with my dog but insists on petting him for a solid minute before I take my seat. Each person I cross I keep my distance from and remain on guard at all times. Anyone could be a mimic. I've learned that the hard way.

Sitting in the very back of the bus, Ammo jumps onto the

seat beside me and lays across my lap with a whine, ears lazy to the sides. I run my hand over his fur to calm not only him but myself.

I can't get the image of that little boy's face out of my head.

It was a mimic. It was a mimic. It was a mimic.

I fight to stay awake for as long as I can. I keep my eyes downcast but aware of everyone in my peripheral vision. Eyes on the floor, my insides are hollow and cold.

I'm so tired.

So empty.

"Good boy," I murmur to Ammo. My head nods, eyes close, and the tears I had been holding back fall onto his fur.

The Past

Sweat gathers on my bare back as the morning sun beats down hot and heavy. Nothing but calm serenity surrounds me. Song birds sing their tunes high up in the pines and birches. A gentle breeze brings blissful comfort against the rising humidity. The stream before me bubbles and churns, its cold water refreshing against my hands as I scrub my dirty and battered shirt. After trekking through these woods for nigh on a week now, it's in need of a good cleaning. I wring out the worn fabric and hold it up to inspect it in the sunshine. There's a couple of holes in the left sleeve where a wendigo landed a lucky swipe of its claws across my arm. At least I got the blood out. I glower at the holes. I'll need to darn them later.

I don't like throwing things out no matter how battered they get. It burns my insides to just throw things away and replace them. Not when things can be fixed.

Unlike so many other things that people throw away.

With a sigh, I wring it out once more and lay it over a rock to dry in the sun for what little time it can. In the meantime, I stretch out beside the stream, ankles crossed over each other and leaning backwards with my arms propped up on the smooth stones. I close my eyes and tilt my face towards the sunlight.

It's so peaceful here.

I do my best to soak it in and not let the thought of tomorrow ruin this moment. I ought to be happy about it. Tomorrow I'll turn eighteen and at last have access to my trust fund free and clear of my uncle's control.

But it's my birthday and . . . I hate it.

Something's clearly wrong in my head for me to think such things—as my uncle likes to remind me—but every time it comes round, I'm on edge. Even now, just the thought of it and my muscles tense up, my hands curl into fists, and my face pulls into a taut frown. I know why. Oh, I certainly know why. That doesn't really make it any easier. Just more frustrating that I can't seem to stop my reaction. Every birthday I can remember was a tug of war match between my parents. They vied over who got to hold the celebration, who was doing a better job of being a parent, whose presents I liked better, and on and on. My birthday has never been about me. Not that I'm a narcissist. I know the world doesn't revolve around me—or gives a crap about me, really. But tomorrow . . . it's the bundled up quintessence of repressed feelings for seeking acceptance from those who are too blind to see it or care.

I stretch my fingers out of their rigid state. Maybe I'll have to find a book on meditation or ways to force yourself to relax.

Footsteps over loose stone and a chuckle stir me out of my reverie.

"You know, it's just going to get dirty again."

A shadow blocks out the sunlight and I open my eyes to Uncle Laurence standing over me with hands planted at his waist and a twisted smirk on his face. He eyes my drying shirt with disdain and a quick roll of the eyes. As if it's stupid of me to want to be in clean clothes. His, meanwhile, are a filthy mess. But he probably won't wash them. It's too much effort. He'll just drag them through the mud, beat the crap out of them, and then toss them away in exchange for a freshly bought set. Use and throw away. I don't have the same methodology but I also don't have the same means. He doesn't like "spending my future fortune" on such meager things as new clothes for me. I have to make them last . . . and then he ridicules me for it. All the while, he splurges on ammo and weapons and things that suit his fancy as my appointed trustee until I come of age.

Until tomorrow.

I don't rise to his taunts and remain silent as I pick up my shirt, flap it a few times for good measure, and tug it back on. The damp fabric feels a bit clingy against my skin yet also cool when the breeze passes through it.

I can be patient. I can lie in wait. I've learned more than combat skills and history during my travels with Uncle Laurence. He's a clever man but so am I.

"We should keep going," he says and shields his eyes from the rising sun to look into the distance. "The hunt's almost over. We're close."

The wendigos we came across were a fluke if anything and not our true prey. No, we've been tracking a rogue werewolf through the forests of the Appalachian Mountains. I had been training at the underwater base off the coast of Virginia for a time—left to my own devices once again—but my uncle returned three months ago insisting on an extended field mission. The timing didn't elude me. Three months from when his powers over my trust end. My uncle could only have two motivations by bringing me along on his secluded adventures. First, he could attempt to persuade me to gift him a significant share of the trust funds by hoodwinking me into thinking we're bonding.

Second, he could very well try to kill me and make it look like an accident.

I know my uncle well enough to at least consider the notion. There's no affection for me but he does enjoy the benefits of substantial funds and the lifestyle it affords him. And it would be so easy to say a monster got the best of me and leave my corpse to rot in some forgotten stretch of woods.

It's taken me some time, but I've finally learned that family doesn't really mean anything at all. No, the most family has ever gotten me is pain, deceit, and lies.

Together we walk back to our camp a little further up the stream hidden in a copse of trees. My things are already bundled up and ready in my hiking pack. I look to my uncle and he gives me a smile. He's been making small efforts like this here and there. It annoys me more than anything. He never does anything for me unless it benefits him somehow. In this case, I would assume he's attempting to bond for the sake of possible trust funds.

Ignoring the hopeful glances he casts my way, I grab my pack, make sure to kick extra dirt over our campfire site, and then wait for him to lead the way. I've been chewed out too many times for taking initiative to head out first, as if it undermines his authority. He checks his gun—not the standard issue bio-mech from the IMS but a .45 he prefers to use. Once a round is racked into the chamber, he nods and walks through the trees. I follow several steps behind, touching a hand to the silver knife I always have hidden on me to reassure myself—a memento of my first horrific monster hunt with my uncle.

Now having a good amount of experience performing hunts such as these, we hardly make a sound as we move and are alert to signs of passage created by our prey. Werewolves aren't nearly as adept at traversing the forest terrain as a normal wolf would be. They tend to leave obvious clues from poorly hidden campsites to blood trails and so on. This one's been more clever than most, however. Probably because this one used to work in the woods for a living as a park ranger. Thomas Howe. He was bitten while on the job and then went psycho, going on a murder spree even with the serum injections that are supposed to keep him in his right mind. Maybe he was never right in the head. Or maybe becoming a werewolf makes some people snap. Whatever the case, he's a menace that needs to be stopped. But, as usual, we're on our own for this hunt. Uncle Laurence has always preferred it that way, and most of the local agents are busy with some other business in Kentucky.

Uncle Laurence gestures silently to me and points to a set of paw prints in the wet soil near a small stream. Clear. Distinct. The first outright mistake the werewolf has made.

An obvious trap.

We share a nod of agreement as he's come to the same conclusion I have.

Despite the evidence before us, we continue on the trail as if oblivious to the trap waiting to be sprung on us. Let the wolf spring it. It'll save us the time of continuing to track it and put an end to this hunt. Whatever the wolf has planned, we can counter it. He doesn't know what *I* can do.

The clear trail of tracks—in earth that should not be this moist—leads down a slope, through a rocky ravine, and comes at last to a narrow cave opening. Nothing can be seen except darkness. An easy way to put us at a disadvantage but also one to turn the tables on him. In almost perfect unison, my uncle and I unstrap our packs and settle them on the trampled ground before the cave entrance. I remove a flare from my pack and hold it at the ready.

Uncle Laurence holds up his hand and counts down on his fingers. At the count of three, I pop the flare and toss it deep into the cave. My uncle swings in first with his .45 raised and I follow in on his tail with his bio-mech gun in my hands.

I expect to find the werewolf outlined by the light of the flare ready to spring. Instead, there's a young woman in ragged, dirty clothes on all fours on the ground. Her face is twisted up in pain and she squints at us with tear streaks through the dirt on her cheeks. A captive? There had been no signs of someone else traveling with or being forcibly taken by the werewolf.

I hesitate and stop breathing all together. An image of another woman pops into my head—my mother crying and bleeding on the ground after being attacked by the werewolf that turned her.

Which is precisely when our werewolf attacks my completely open right side from out of the shadows. The thunderous boom of a gunshot is deafening inside the cave and the world is a flurry of jaws and claws, screams and shouts. I'm knocked to the ground, my arm burns, and my eyes dart to the only light nearby—the flare and the woman beside it screaming. I blur through time and space to reappear at her side. I throw an arm out to shield her and hold her back as Uncle Laurence swivels out of the werewolf's way when it leaps for him. When the werewolf lands, my uncle pins it with his sights and empties his clip into the monster.

The smell of blood and gunpowder fills the air of the small cave. The werewolf doesn't get back up. The women continues to scream and grabs my arm, clinging onto me in a death grip.

"You're okay," I say forcefully over the tremendous sound she's making. "It's over. Freaking out is *not* helping yourself."

I try to tug her off my arm and pat her on the back at the same time. It's what you're supposed to do for a distressed person. Assure them with physical attentions like a friendly back pat.

She angles about so her eyes catch the dying light of the flare. The yellow rims around her irises are like wheels of fire. The sound of her screams begin to change in pitch. Her teeth lengthen into canines.

"Help me!" she shrieks as her body blossoms with dark fur.

Heaven's above, she's been bitten.

"Charlie!" my uncle shouts.

Another voice echoes in my head like a thousand thunderbolts hitting the earth.

Charlie! Help me, Charlie!

Mom bloody and sobbing and reaching out to me. Rain cascading down her face. Rain drumming on the roof of the car. Thunder cracking in the distance. My hands won't stop shaking. Her hands shake too. Why won't they stop shaking? Why doesn't someone help her?

A gunshot ends the screams both in my head and surrounding me.

Then there's blood. Real blood. Not imagined. It covers my hands as it gushes out of the hole in the woman's chest. Her yellow-rimmed eyes plead with me to save her, accuse me of this terrible fate. Her body sags until those haunting eyes close and she hangs limp in my arms.

I can't breathe.

"You okay, Charlie?"

My voice is small when I try to speak. "She can . . . she can still heal. Werewolves, they—"

"She won't."

But we—we could have saved her. We *should* have.

Help me, Charlie!

Rage like a living thing takes over. The poor woman falls to the floor and I rise to my feet. My uncle holds out a hand as if to soothe me—a laughable attempt. I move right around him to the body of the werewolf on the floor.

My foot connects with it's bullet-riddled chest. A madman's shout of anger leaves my mouth as I kick again and again, blood covering my shoes and pants.

"Charlie—"

I sink to my knees to start swinging my fists, pounding every inch of his despicable, worthless body that I can reach. Unintelligible grunts leave me as fist meets flesh—left, right, left, right, left, right. That woman died because of him! Because of his disgusting, infuriating—

"*Charlie.*"

I'm blind and the pain in my knuckles only makes me want to punch harder, to punish him for what he did. I hope he feels every hit in whatever hell he's ended up in. I want him to know. I want him to *feel* it. This rage eats me up from the inside and has every day since a werewolf just like him cursed my mom and signed her death warrant. Now someone else's mother, sister, daughter, or wife has been taken away from people that love her. People that don't know what they'll do without her.

"CHARLIE."

A hand grabs my arm and pulls me back from another punch.

"You're just making wine at this point," my uncle says. "Keep going like that and you're going to poison yourself with his blood. He's dead. Knock it off."

In a singular motion, I twist up onto my feet, swing around with my blood-soaked fist, and hit him square in the jaw. He stumbles into the side of the cave and presses the back of his hand to the side of his face.

"YOU SHOT HER!" I roar. "WE COULD HAVE GIVEN HER THE SERUM!"

He pushes himself upright. "She was going to bite you! I saved your hide!"

"YOU BASTARD!"

This time he launches at me, gun tossed aside and fists raised. I don't port away but let him come at me. We get our arms around each other and stumble around trying to get the upper hand on one another. I manage to break free and it's a series of throwing jabs and blocking punches. I hit him a few more times round the face and he gives me a puffy lip along with a sharp hit to the ribs.

He shoves off of me. "ENOUGH!"

Panting and slightly hunched as my ribs ache, I shout back, "You're right! I've had enough! Enough of you to last a lifetime and then some. I *never* want to see you again."

"You need me, you greasy little runt! Without me, you would've been dead ages ago."

"Without you, I'd still have a mother," I snarl. "I hope you enjoyed the benefits of bleeding me dry, *uncle*."

"You little—"

"*This is it*. I'm *done*. I'm done with you, with all of it. I hope you die a long, painful death. It's what you deserve."

"I swear, I'm gonna—"

But I'm already gone. One look over my shoulder and I'm free of the cave. I grab my pack with a grimace and disappear into the forest. I teleport again and again to put as much distance as possible between me and my uncle. With any luck he'll walk right into a famished bear or something. I can only hope.

Out of breath and in a great deal of pain, I finally stop before a shallow stream and thrust my hands into the cold water. There's so much blood. It fouls the clean water and trails off my fingers like red smoke to be carried away in the ebbing current. I can hardly bear to rub it off for the pain in my knuckles. As the blood of the werewolf washes away, I can see the damage I inflicted on myself in my manic attack on a dead man. The skin's scratched and scuffed, swollen, and turning colors already.

The rage still boils beneath but the cold water starts to take that away too. Leaving only despair and self-loathing behind.

I remain at the stream for some time and examine my shirt with disdain now soiled with blotches of blood.

Closing my eyes, I lift my face to the sun and let the breeze take away the burning heat in my cheeks. None of the peace I found this morning returns beneath the bright sunlight. But there is certainty. I'm never going back to my uncle ever again, no matter what he says. From this moment on, I'm going to be free. Free of my uncle. Free of caring. Free of relationships that always end in pain.

I'll be alone. The thought of it . . . hurts.

But nothing can be worse than the pain in my bones right now.

Present Day
Part 6

The trip to Dreamland is a slow journey but with Ammo by my side, I have some level of warning if the mimics try to attack me again. To my surprise, they don't. But he won't warn me of police which I'm sure are also on the lookout for me. I try to stay alert as much as possible but I also use the long bus ride to sleep and rest as much as I can. I hop between buses every so often to throw any trackers off my trail. A few times I have to convince the driver that Ammo is a service dog in order to keep him with me. Not everyone is so pleased to have an eighty-pound German Shepherd sharing their bus. I split my meals with him so he's happy enough to continue to tag along.

I wonder what his owners thought when they came home to their dog missing and a pair of corpses in their hallway.

Unless I actually killed the owners.

The thought keeps coming back to haunt me and hollow out my insides. I swear I saw black eyes. But what if I only saw what I wanted to see? What if it was a trick of the light? I massage my forehead and give Ammo a good scratch behind the ears.

The true power of the mimics isn't their ability to copy but to confuse. I've been hunting monsters a long time now. More than once I've had moments of questioning the morality of my actions but this has been the worst by far. The continuous doubt chews me up.

Ammo licking my hands and laying his head in my lap has a strangely comforting effect on me that tides me through the dark eddies of thoughts. I've never had a pet before. I don't count the beta fish my mother got me once when I was very young. I only had it for a month. The tank got pretty dirty but I wasn't sure how to clean it by myself. My mother didn't know either and my father didn't want to help. Tiny George ended up getting flushed down a toilet. To this day I'm not sure which of my parents did it. I named that fish after my grandfather, again someone I only knew briefly. He was a warm and generous person but died with my grandmother in a car accident shortly after spending Christmas with us for the last time. It was that Christmas he gave my mother his bracelet. She wore it all the time until gifting it to my father—a significant move on her part. If only it had done more for both of them.

I lean my head back against the seat and stare out the window at the brown land and bare trees flashing past.

The people I care about never last long in my life—Grandpa and Grandma, Dad, then Mom, the few scattered friends I managed to make. They always leave me in the end, one way or another. And that deep ache I carry in my chest every day has been a constant reminder of why it's easier to simply not make those connections at all in the first place.

It's easier being alone.

I don't mind being alone.

But I don't really fancy it either.

The journey south takes me through a couple downpours, late season storms, and a cold snap, across long, long stretches of boring plains, through beautiful snow-capped mountains, and at last to the dry heat and sand of Nevada. I stare out the windows at the rolling desert, the bare trees, the dense shrubs. Being back here brings a share of memories with it, some very painful.

And now I know somewhere out there is also the Fields. A *reconditioning* facility for werewolves. I didn't see the videos my team did of what happened there, but Alona explained enough to turn my stomach. It twists even now thinking about it and what Merlin endured there—what Phoenix would be forced to endure if she had successfully turned herself in.

That future is still on the horizon. There will be a lot to do before then but . . . the day is coming when she'll walk into dark halls like those and never come back out.

I had been angry at her for hiding what she could do. I couldn't comprehend why she would hide such gifts.

What I wouldn't do to take back the words I said.

Ammo gives a dramatic sigh on the seat beside me and I press my forehead against the window.

In the far distance I espy the top of a dust cloud along the craggy mountains. We're almost there.

After another half hour, we reach the large bus terminal

that marks the end of the line for this mode of transportation. Ammo hops off the seat and does a little dog yoga as I stretch my stiff legs. I take care when we exit the bus and enter a relatively crowded area. It's hard to tell if anyone is watching me specifically since so many people stop to look or fawn over Ammo. There are advantages and disadvantages to the dog trotting along at my side.

And while Ammo might be my first line of defense against any monsters in the crowd, he gives me no warning of the police officers that covertly shoulder their way towards me. I've already picked out the exits and veer for the closest one. I'm halfway across the tiles of the terminal when I spot another officer hiding in the shadow of the open doorway. Over my shoulder, the others are nearly upon me from behind. A glance at the ceiling tells me there are no camera blindspots. There's only one option open to me.

I stop and bend down to Ammo's height, bracing hands on both of his shoulders. His warm breath blows in my face, completely at ease and unaware of what's going on. I hope he doesn't bite me for what happens next.

Even when the officers nearly have me surrounded, I wait for a pack of travelers to swarm around me towards the exit. Bent low with their bodies hiding me from view of both the officers and cameras, I focus on the exit on the far side of the building. I almost lose sight of it between the legs of the people around me but I only need a split second.

I vanish out of the closing net and reappear on the far side with Ammo still grasped between my hands. However, as for everyone except Phoenix that's joined me on a teleportation, the dog invariably suffers the potent pain of my magic. He lets out a sharp, high-pitched whine and does in fact go to snap at my arm. I jerk my hand out of the way and hold his muzzle closed tight in both hands. He struggles and flails a bit so I let go. But he doesn't bark again. Only twitches and acts very on edge as if that phantom pain will strike again. I certainly hope I don't have to resort to porting again. My body aches with it.

"I'm sorry, boy," I murmur and give him a quick head rub before hurrying out of the terminal with him.

If those officers know I'm here, then it's only a matter of time before an IMS agent is notified. They could be waiting for me by the time I reach Dreamland. I need to hurry and reach the city before that happens. Something easier said than done.

I keep on walking, putting as much distance between me and the terminal as possible. Having Ammo at my side sort of makes me stick out like a sore thumb but I can't afford to separate at this point—that, and I'd feel terribly guilty just ditching the poor guy after everything we've gone through.

Despite the risk, I have no choice but to hail the mirage bus for a ride into Dreamland. The only other way into the city would be hiking through the desert, hoping I don't get spotted by the perimeter guard, and somehow making it to The Shroud entrance the gryphons use. That's a bad idea all around so I'd rather risk the bus. Well, technically all of this is a bad idea but I don't have much choice. Scholar's never reappeared and the gryphons are the best shot I have for allies at the moment.

Heading for the paved road that splits the sprawling desert in two, I walk along the shoulder and stick out my hand to signal the bus. My fingers curve to form a lowercase "d" unlike the usual thumbs up hitchhikers use for a ride. I keep my arm extended with that symbol. The bus will come by at some point but it'll be hard to spot—that's the point though. Ammo walks beside me with his head hanging low, tongue lolling out, and his panting a steady beat. A few stray cars pass us but no police, thankfully. It won't be long though until I'm spotted. I'm an open and visible target. Too vulnerable. I don't like it.

Then . . .

There. The heat rising from the pavement shifts and morphs as if a mirage has begun to move across it. I wave my curved fingers in the air a bit to make sure I have its attention. The strange shimmering draws ever closer until I can just barely make out the shape of a bulky bus within it, a transparent ghost on the road. I step off the side of the pavement and the mirage halts directly before me until I, too, am swallowed up by the illusion. One step forward and the bus appears out of thin air. I glance to the group of sprites—fire, air, water, and earth—squatting on top of the white roof and spinning the mirage illusion around the bus. They peer at me curiously but their attention is mainly fixated on maintaining the illusionary cover.

Ammo starts to huff, like a whispered bark.

I don't know if he's reacting to the magical creatures before him or if he senses something more sinister on the bus. I hesitate before making for the open door and holding Ammo's leash taut as he tries to race forward, sniffing everything frantically. At first glance it looks as if a tree is planted in the driver's seat, a branch grasping the door mechanism and another on the wheel. But I see the brilliant green eyes through the foliage. A desert willow nymph. The tree morphs just enough to have the shape of a woman dressed in pink blossoms, sandy bark, and vine-like greenery. She offers me a smile.

Ammo starts barking like crazy. I have to drag him back

when he tries licking—or heavens forbid *biting*—the nymph bus driver. Her smile fades a bit. I toss appropriate fare into the payment bucket and move past her, struggling to keep Ammo in check.

He doesn't stop barking at everyone and everything on the bus. A pair of spirit walker coyotes openly stare, a unicorn snorts in my direction, and a faun dressed like a goth eyes me with suspicion. I grit my teeth as I take a seat near the back and glare at Ammo.

"You're *not* helping now," I hiss at him.

The downside of having Ammo becomes glaringly obvious. He doesn't seem keen on stopping his barking anytime soon either. Cheeks burning, I keep my gaze on the window as I continuously hiss at him to be quiet and tug on his leash. He's calling all sorts of attention to us which is exactly what I don't want. Maybe I should have left him at the bus terminal. Surely someone would have checked his tag and contacted his owners. He would have been fine.

It was stupid of me to have formed an attachment to the dog.

The other travelers keep throwing me nasty glares but the one faun doesn't glare at the dog or me. No, she stares with wide eyes as if terrified. Maybe she's afraid of dogs. They clearly don't react well to strange magical creatures.

After at least five minutes on the bus, Ammo finally settles down and shuts up. I do my best to keep him quiet with pats and quiet assurances. I'll let him go as soon as I'm able since I've almost reached my goal. Just a few—but very problematic—hurdles left.

The bus rumbles along and I get side-eye glances from the driver in the rearview mirror. I wonder if the nymph knows who I am. There's bound to be a warrant out for my arrest and wanted photos. I'm not sure my disguise is working anymore now that I'm back in the magical realm. Everyone tends to pay better attention to the small details. Especially fauns. The gaze of the faun goth is starting to irritate me. I've never liked being around them. They're too keen on the emotions of others with their empathetic abilities. They always see right through me. It's like I'm laid bare and no mask I don can convince them otherwise of the turmoil, pain, and doubt within. I hate it.

I ignore the faun as best I can as a gentle tinkling sound echoes through the bus over loudspeakers moments before we enter the swirling cover of the dust storm that hides the main shuttle entrance. The constant cloud is all that can be seen through the windows and the light gradually grows darker and darker. We reach a tunnel leading down into the earth and the storm immediately dissipates. Twenty seconds later we reach the shuttle bay for the mirage buses under bright floodlights. Guards stand at the lifts and patrol the bay. The driver glances back at me again and I notice more guards than usual waiting for our bus in particular as it pulls to a stop before the cement pad leading to the lifts.

Ammo peers up at me as I unhook his leash and give him a final scratch behind the ears.

"You've been a good boy," I murmur. "I need you to do one last thing for me."

The doors to the bus open. The unicorn trots forward followed by the others. The faun hesitates before rising to exit as well. I wait until the corridor is filled and the guards have moved to the doors. Then I wrap a hand in Ammo's fur and port us across the bay to the back of another bus.

Ammo yips loudly at the pain and I immediately let him go as I port to the front of another bus on the opposite side of the bay. The guards start scanning the area where Ammo is barking while I get an angle on the open elevator doors. I wait until the men posted there are looking towards the commotion before porting directly inside the elevator and quickly pressing up against the short bit of wall between me and the guards. I suck in a sharp breath and tightly press a hand to my side at the intense pain there.

I wait for others to filter in to hide amongst but the guards are stopping any passengers from entering until they figure out what's going on. Well, there goes my cover of a crowd. After a quick check on the men now busy holding off an irritable uni-corn, I hit the button and the doors begin to close. There's only a small gap left when the goth faun from the bus slips in. The doors close behind her, shutting out the muffled sounds of the guards realizing the lift is in motion.

The faun and I stare at each other from either side of the lift as it begins to lower.

"Hello," she says quietly.

I don't say anything.

"It's customary to say hello in return," she says.

"Well, I don't really care, so ..."

"Is it because you're in pain?" She gestures to my hand pressed against my side.

I level a flat glare at her. "Conversations with strangers are more painful. Especially persistent, annoying strangers."

She gives me a frosty gaze of her own. "Rude."

A little two-fingered salute in her direction has her turn her attention to the opposite wall instead of me. Once her eyes are no longer inspecting me, I sag against the cold metal behind me and hang my head. I'm so very tired and no longer have Ammo to rely on.

The lift picks up speed and we travel story after story deeper into the earth. The external heat shifts into pleasant coolness. I enjoy it for as much as I can, for this short respite before the next difficult step.

My eyes shift to the faun. Her hair has been dyed black with bright pink and purple stripes hiding underneath. The colors seem to trail from her hair and across the top of her furry shoulders in swirls and whorls. It must be some artistic fad with the fauns or something. She's also forgone the usual brocade favored by her people for a heavy black fabric studded with chrome spikes around her throat and adorning her wrists. But beneath that heavily laden exterior, I see her hands shaking slightly, her eyes darting between the front and back doors of the elevator, see her glancing at the indicator above our heads showing just how deep we are.

I consider my own dark eyeliner, the blue I've put in my hair, the searching glances I've been making.

She's on the run like me. That doesn't necessarily mean she's running from people trying to kill her. It could be anything. People are always running from something, whether it be commitment, denied emotions, family, relationships, or their past.

My eyes slide away. It takes one to know one, and I'm an expert.

The elevator goes far enough that the grated windows

facing the interior of Dreamland stop showing metal walls flashing past and open up to the huge chasm of the city lurking deep beneath Nevada. Between the slits I see the great Pit in the very center surrounded by golden columns embellished with gryphon carvings, the wide atrium walkways, balconies, and split passageways. Red and orange rock form most of the foundations, walls, and ceilings of this place, giving it a persistent warm glow. I step closer to the grates and grip the interior railing as my eyes catch on the aerie directly opposite the lifts. Great semi-circles are carved into the bedrock to house the host of gryphons that live here. The aerie rises in levels on the other side of the Pit filled with shifting feathers and gleaming armor I can make out even from this distance. Through the back of those sprawling aeries is the Shroud—the entrance and exit for aerial creatures and vehicles, constantly camouflaged by a dust storm and illusion made by the sprites.

It's where I need to go. It's also a lot farther away than it appears.

The lift gives a shudder when we're still a good fifty feet from the floor. I'm too suspicious of everything now to dismiss it as a normal elevator hiccup. I keep a slight bend in my knees, a hand still braced on the railing, as my body tenses up. There's a sudden sharp drop and halt that has me swaying. The faun locks eyes for a split second and I sense her fear. She skitters over to the other grate looking over the city and grabs the railing as well.

A mighty screech echoes through the metal tube.

My stomach flies up into my throat as the elevator starts to free fall.

Definitely not a normal hiccup in function.

Instincts drive me into action. I immediately hunt for the closest spot to safely teleport out of here.

The grates on the elevator begin to close to block out my view.

I slam a fist against the shutters but they don't budge. Mere seconds stand between the elevator and rock bottom. But if I can't see, then I can't get us out of this death trap. Maybe I could port us in the air right when we crash, but I can't calculate those odds at precisely the right moment to make it work—

A cloven hoof slams into the shutters and breaks a slat. I can see the reddish floor rising up to meet us. Without even thinking, I grab hold of the faun's arm and will us to move. Sucked through time and space, we hit the ground hard and roll. A split second later the lift slams into the base behind us with a horrendous crash and screeching of metal. The shudder of the impact goes through me and I throw an arm over the faun as a cloud rises to engulf everything within a thirty foot radius.

Pain radiates up through my side and I breathe through clenched teeth. A coughing fit takes me as dust from the crash whirls around us. Blinking through the thinning cloud, I survey what would have been my fate if I had been just a second too slow. Bent metal, broken stone, and sparks.

"I thought you didn't care," the faun under my protection says breathlessly.

"I'm anti-social," I cough. "Not heartless."

Screams and shouts rend the air in the aftermath of the crash. I push myself up despite the agony in my body and spot a crowd of IMS agents charging towards us. The faun grabs my arm and gives me big doe eyes painted with fear.

Definitely on the run then, not from emotions or family but *them*.

"I hope you're not afraid of heights," I say.

I lift my eyes to the center of the city.

We vanish.

And reappear over the gaping maw of the Pit.

The faun screams as we begin to plummet into darkness.

My stomach twists unpleasantly as the air whips past my face. I draw out my arms and legs to provide some resistance to slow the fall but the faun tumbles and flails to the point I almost lose my hold on her arm. I try to shout at her to hold still but I don't think she hears me in her panic. I guess I should have given her more of a warning.

Past the whistling wind in my ears, the mighty down thrust of wings comes rising out of the darkness. A sharp, golden beak emerges into the light followed by glistening feathers on wings that span twice my height and then some. Black talons stretch up towards us as we come rushing down. Just as I knew would happen.

The sharp jerk as the gryphon wraps a sinewy foot around my upper arm rips a cry of pain from me. I manage to keep my grip on the faun and she dangles beneath me continuing to scream.

The gryphon flaps its thunderous wings to steady itself and hover midair. A great, gleaming eye peers down at me relentlessly—judging me and irritated to be sure. Only idiots come falling down here.

"I seek the sanctuary of General Bakari," I shout to be heard over the faun. "The IMS has been compromised."

The Past

It's been nearly a year since I joined the Duluth Field Office and this stupid Agent Melody Boyd still will not leave me alone. I feel like no matter what I do or say, she's always there offering peppy advice and trying to be friendly. It's annoying and I want her to stop. When I wake up, she asks if I want eggs. When we go out on our daily errands, she offers to buy me coffee. When I snap at her to leave me alone, she quietly asks if I want to talk. I swear, the woman's never heard of personal space.

Then there's Agents Chip Bodash and Rodney Nelson. Bodash is built like a bear and looks like one too with hairy arms and a puffy beard. He talks like I imagine a bear would as well—a real deep, scratchy kind of voice. But he's as big a marshmallow as Boyd. Nelson isn't much better. Chatty yet soft-spoken and a living breathing string bean if ever I saw one. At least he's left me alone since I called him an idiot during our first meeting. Now if I could only get the other two to stop trying to pry into my business . . .

Things have only gotten worse lately. I've been counting down the days. It's my birthday today. Something dark and deadly has been coiling in my chest in anticipation as it always does. I'm more on edge than usual and pointedly ignore Boyd's sideways looks as we walk through Canal Park on our usual patrol to check the bay entrances. She doesn't try to chat which is perfectly fine by me. Instead we perform our duties in silence which I prefer. Around lunch time, I split off to get my own food away from her and to enjoy a moment of privacy if possible. Unfortunately, during this time of year the city is packed with tourists and sightseers. I grab a burger and try to hide on the walkway beneath the lift bridge. It's less crowded at least and I have a great view of the waves.

That's when I notice a man in ragged clothes sitting farther down the walkway with a sign that says *Veteran. Will work for food.* There's not a trace of hope or life in his weathered face.

Another person tossed aside and left to waste away.

He glances in my direction and I quickly look down at my food to avoid eye contact. Suddenly I don't feel remotely as hungry as I did before.

That darkness rises up in my chest.

The food's wasted on me anyhow. What use have I been to the world? I'm a sorry, pathetic excuse for a human being. Just a thing that sparked a divorce, ripped apart the lives of my family, and just…existed. What have I done? Nothing. Absolutely nothing. I don't even have the decency to look the veteran in the eye. A coward. A selfish, miserable little—

I wrap up the remnants of my burger with a sigh and walk

away in the opposite direction of the man. Pushing none too gently through irritating tourists, I return to the fast food joint and order the biggest combo they have. When I walk out with a stuffed bag, I stick what's left of my burger in as well and grab an application for restaurant workers off the counter by the door. The entire walk back to the lift bridge, I have to psych myself up. I hate going up to strangers. Or talking to them. Or making eye contact. Or pretending to smile like I give a crap. But I can do this. I'll just leave the bag and walk away. I picture it in my head so I have the steps down.

The veteran is still right where I left him on the walkway. Tourists pass by without a second glance or mutter under their breath. I hesitate for a moment before walking quietly up behind the man and putting the bag down beside him. However, before I can make a swift unobtrusive exit, the man turns around. His eyes go to the bag of food and then to me.

"Thank you," he says softly.

I freeze up before I give him a single nod and hurry away. I keep going until I find a tree I can sort of hide behind. From a distance, I watch the man break into the food. I did something, but it's hardly enough. I should do more. I *could* do more but I'm a coward. I should have offered him some company or . . . I don't know.

"Ready to go?"

I spin around to find Boyd standing there with a soft expression on her face like she wants to pinch my cheeks or something.

My face burns, I clear my throat, and shift from foot to foot. "Let's go."

She spins about on her heel and leads the way with a bounce

in her step. I roll my eyes. I'm in a bad mood and I know it so I try to focus on the remaining tasks for the day. We head to the Blue Comet first. My partner stays outside on the sidewalk while I go in alone to check the lower bar area for any disturbances or situations amongst the mermaids, selkies, elves, and occasional fauns that come through here. Agent Boyd's been banned since the last time she came here, she got into a fight with a selkie that turned into a full out brawl. Real professional. It's the only time I've seen her worked up or, heck, even angry. After a quick check with the bartenders and patrons with nothing to report, I hurry back out before a pair of selkies that have been tailing me can ask me to dance or something. Next, there are a number of werewolves we need to check in on—it's the part of the day I really hate. I want nothing to do with them so I stay in the background as Agent Boyd makes contact to check serum logs and ask the appropriate questions.

We head back to the field office as the sun sets. Agents Bodash and Nelson will be heading out next to cover the night time hours when more of the dangerous and exotic creatures sneak about. There have been rumors of a wendigo possibly hiding along the Superior Hiking Trail. I've been ever so aware of the silver hunting knife always hidden in my pocket. It's my . . . safety blanket, I suppose, from my first true monster hunting experience tangling with a pair of wendigos that almost gutted me. A reminder of yet another one of the terrible memories I'll always have from my time with my uncle.

Upon entering the field office, Agent Bodash passes a letter to me on his way out to start his patrol with Agent Nelson.

"Came in this morning for you," he says by way of greeting. "See you later!"

I don't respond. My eyes are glued to the return address on the corner of the envelope. The blood drains out of my face.

"Everything all right?" Agent Boyd asks.

Ignoring her, I move further into the office to stand by one of the big bay windows and open the letter with shaky fingers. Inside is a small slip of paper with a note scrawled in my uncle's handwriting.

Thinking of you, CJ.

Silence presses in on my ears and I stare at the insufferable little taunt he sent me. He knew exactly what today was and how I feel about it. He just wanted to push me over the edge and remind me that I'll never be free of him. No matter what I do, he'll always be there tormenting me, even from a distance.

"Charlie?"

I spin about on Boyd who's snuck up behind me and shout in her face. "*For once just leave me alone!*"

She blinks.

I crumple the envelope and letter into the smallest possible ball with all my rage and hurl it across the room. I never should have opened it. I should have burned it or torn it to shreds the second it came.

Turning away from Boyd and the room, I make for the stairs.

"*Sit down.*"

I stop and look at her in surprise. She's never used such a thunderous and commanding tone before. Her eyes are narrowed, body rigid and tense as if ready for battle. It's a shock she can actually be intimidating.

"I am the supervising agent in this field office and you are going to *sit down.*" She points to a stool at the eat-in counter of the kitchen. She remains that way until I slowly walk over and take a seat. She moves around to the other side of the counter, crosses her arms over her chest, and stares me down. Fear fogs my brain as I'm reminded of encounters with my uncle. I've pushed the boundaries too far. It's going to happen again, isn't it? The anger, the torment, the loathing. I bring in my shoulders like a helpless little boy again. I hate this feeling but it dogs me like a shadow. Inescapable.

"I didn't want to have to do this but you've left me little choice."

Here it comes.

"Enough's enough, Charlie." She looses a heavy sigh. "*Talk to me.*"

"What?"

"No one carries around that much anger unless they're in pain."

I roll my eyes. "How would you know?"

"Because I've been that angry before. In fact, I still have trouble with it."

"I doubt that," I grumble.

She reaches over the counter and smacks me upside the head. I lean back shocked.

"Hey!"

With both hands planted on the counter top she leans towards me. "Someone needed to do that for me so I'm going to do it for you. It's a sign of affection."

I glower at her. "It's a physical assault."

"Hardly. I used to be a Spartan. I know the difference."

"Wait—what?" She's never mentioned anything like that

before. As far as I knew, she's always been a field agent. And I didn't think anyone's ever *stopped* being a Spartan.

"You heard me."

"But—"

"Let's make a deal," she says. "If I'm open with you, I want you to be open with me. Wounds that go untreated will fester. And you can't heal mental wounds if you don't share the burden with someone. Trust me. I've been there."

"So, you want to play therapist?"

She shakes her head. "I want to be your friend."

My eyes narrow. "Why?"

A sad sort of smile settles on her face. "Because I see myself in you. The only thing that got me through that period of my life was having someone I could talk to."

"I'm not a talkative person."

"I'm not asking you to be." She raps her fingers on the counter. "You know, what? Why don't I start?" She drags a stool over to sit opposite me then clasps her hands together on the counter. "For starters . . . I'm a selkie. At least, I used to be."

It takes a couple moments for it to sink in—and for me to understand what she's truly saying. There's only one way she could say she *used* to be a selkie. All selkies possess a magical skin that allows them to transform from seal to woman. Without it . . .

"You're a hollow," I say quietly.

She nods and anxiously fiddles with her fingers. "During my time as a Spartan, my team was ambushed and separated. I . . . it was . . ." She swallows as if the memory is still too painful to talk about. "I went to rescue my comrades. In the process, my skin was stolen from me. I was left with a choice. Save my skin and magic, or save my teammates. So . . . my skin was burned and my magic ripped from me. But by that sacrifice, I managed to save the others and escape. After that I . . . I couldn't stay with the Spartans. I was too bitter and eaten up by anger. The very essence of who I was had been stripped away from me. I can still feel it like a phantom limb."

"There's nothing that can be done?"

"No. Once it's lost, it's lost forever."

I can't begin to imagine what that would be like. Who would I be without the magic in my blood? It's become so much a part of me that having it taken away would break me entirely.

She rolls her lips and traces an invisible pattern on the counter with her fingertip. "I left the Spartans and asked for a field agent position instead. I couldn't take on that increased danger each day with the state I was in. I became depressed. I felt as if I couldn't do a single thing right, that there was no point to my life or living anymore. And when the sense of worthlessness became too much, I'd have nasty fits of rage and lash out at anyone around me. Those days still haunt me."

Heat crawls up my neck. I know exactly what that feels like on a daily basis. That *is* me. Every day. Every waking hour. Every blasted second.

"How did . . ." I clear my throat and find it very difficult to ask such a personal thing. "How did you overcome it?"

"It wasn't easy. But I found friends to support me. Chip and Rodney have helped a great deal. And ... I was on anti-depressants for some time. That, along with talking about it with someone who wouldn't judge, only listen, helped enormously." She finally looks up again to meet my eyes. "Which is why I'm not giving up on you, Charlie. I want to be that person for you because I see you going through the same pain I did. I'm asking you to trust me, even if just a little. I want to help."

I'm about to respond with a snappish retort but stop myself. No one simply wants to help other people. There's always an end goal and something in it for them. And yet . . . I can't help but trust her after what she's confessed. She's always tried to be helpful for the sake of others and has never given me reason to believe otherwise.

Maybe if I had reached out to someone earlier—like General Bakari—my life would have turned out much differently. If I had confronted my parents. If I hadn't remained with my uncle. If I could only *trust* someone as I so desperately want to.

A leap of faith. Like the gryphons when they train. You can't learn to fly if you never take that first plunge.

"You don't have to tell me everything," she continues. "Not unless you want to. I don't want you to feel pressured, but this—this intense *anger* can't control you as it did today. You can't work for the IMS like this and you certainly can't live your life that way either."

I honestly don't know what to say.

"When you want to talk," she says softly, "you know where to find me."

The only thing I can do is nod. My mouth is dry and my throat shut tight. She stands and leaves me at the eat-in counter.

"Oh, but before I forget—" She comes back around holding a small wrapped present and sets it in front of me. "Happy birthday, Charlie."

She knows? Instead of hovering around waiting for me to open it—like my parents used to—she let's me open it in peace alone as she disappears down the stairs to the level below. The dimensions of the gift make it obvious what's inside. I rip off the wrapping paper and find a book. *The Mote in God's Eye* by Larry Niven.

A book. One I haven't read yet either. Not a useless or thoughtless gift. No, she paid attention. She noticed how often and much I read. Then she went out of her way to get me a gift on my birthday. My uncle couldn't claim to do the same, nor even my parents.

I clutch onto the book as if it's made of solid gold.

Maybe—just maybe—I might be ready to trust someone again.

Still holding onto the dear present, I take the stairs to the lower level, walk down the hallway, and knock on the open door to Agent Boyd's room. She's sitting on the edge of her bed with a report in her hands, but looks up immediately as if she had been waiting for me.

"Melody," I say. It's the first time I've ever called her by her first name and she smiles.

"Charlie."

I hold the book tight to my chest as if I could use it as a shield to guard my heart. "I've never had a real family—or at least, one that acted like it. My uncle raised me after my parents' were killed, but he didn't want to. I've never been wanted. Or liked. And I . . . I don't even know how to say thank you properly for a birthday present. Or had one without strings attached." My throat constricts and I find my voice cracking. What a stupid, stupid thing to do. I clear my throat and try to regain some of my composure. "What I'm trying to say is . . . I don't know how to talk with people or have friends or *be* a friend. But—"

I blow out a breath and stare down the hallway.

"But?" she asks quietly.

"But I want to." I summon my courage to look her in the face once more. There's nothing but warmth and light there. No judging. No sneer. Just . . . a friend. "Can we talk?"

Present Day
Part 7

The gryphon sweeps up out of the great Pit in the middle of Dreamland and deposits me and the faun a bit roughly on the hard stone at the top. We're immediately surrounded by IMS agents with bio-mech guns aimed and ready. The gryphon takes off, deserting us.

I raise my hands to either side of my head but the faun remains on all fours shaking. I want to scooch away from her in case she vomits but with those guns aimed at my head, I'd rather not make any move that might provoke them to fire.

A crowd gathers behind the agents.

"That's Charlie Jaeger," one of the agents says to the others. Not *Spartan* Charlie Jaeger—as if I've been stripped of my hard-earned title already. I grit my teeth.

A woman stalks through the agents in a pristine navy suit,

blonde hair pulled back from her severe expression. Her eyes are cold, her stance rigid.

Director Dunham.

"Charlie Jaeger, you are hereby under arrest for sedition, treason, and murder," she says with her focus on me. "No sudden moves or we will be compelled to use deadly force."

I knew they were presenting false charges for being a traitor, but murder now too?

She only casts a cursory glance at the faun—who's now glaring fiercely at the director. I don't think I've ever seen a faun look so incensed before. I hardly even see them mad.

"And how exactly did I manage to do all that from a hospital bed?" I ask cooly. "Half the time unconscious at that. Was I supposedly conspiring against the IMS with that lamia when I took a bullet to the chest?"

"We've been given clear and convincing evidence from a very reliable source. Don't expect to talk yourself out of this one. Head down and keep your hands where they are."

"If you'll look behind me, you'll find some clear and convincing evidence that someone's currently trying to kill me. To keep me quiet and label me as a patsy."

More than one person looks to the destruction of the elevator.

"Clever to use a freak accident in your defense," the director says without the slightest bit of inflection. "Head down and hands where they are. *Now.*"

I don't move.

She gestures to one of the men beside her. "Take him down and hold him in the penitent cells."

In the distance, there are several airy booms.

I smirk. "That's not going to happen."

The agents shift their focus from me to something overhead. Moments later, a host of gryphons touch down on the stone floor. Rocking me with the downdraft of his wings, General Bakari lands between the agents and me acting as a shield. His golden feathery ears stand straight and he holds his wings slightly aloft to look bigger than he already is.

"They have asked for sanctuary," the general intones, his low voice echoing through the huge chamber. "On my honor as a gryphon, I am obliged to accept and guard them with my life until such a time we revoke their status as wards."

The director bristles. "The IMS has sole authority in the jurisdiction of criminals issued warrants by our agency."

"Not according to section thirteen of the Dragon Pact," I say and can't help but smile. "Gryphons are afforded certain acts of territorial immunity. Harboring those seeking sanctuary is one of them."

"I beg to differ," she snarls.

A chorus of clicking beaks and talons scrapping on the stone cut off any argument she might fire back. Bakari's feathers bristle with indignation. Gryphons are proud. Trying to undermine their rights is a grave mistake. One Director Dunham should know intimately since she's been stationed here for years in charge of gryphon territory.

If she's Director Dunham at all.

At a swiped gesture from the general, several gryphons stalk forward and the agents back up to give them room.

"Come." The general flicks a feathered tail at me and gracefully walks towards the aerie.

I push to my feet with a grimace and the faun beside me does the same to follow after the general. We walk side by side through the silence now filling Dreamland that's followed swiftly by fevered whispers.

"Who *are* you?" the faun asks sharply.

"Pretty sure they said my name a few times," I say. "Who are *you*?"

"Talia. They said you committed murder and treason."

"People say crap all the time. Doesn't make it true."

"There's a warrant for your arrest," she continues. "You asked for sanctuary. You're on the *run*."

"So are you," I fire back. "Anyone can see that. Instead of questioning me nonstop, maybe you should thank me for saving your hide."

"You mean for tossing me into a bottomless pit thinking I was going to die?"

I roll my eyes. "This is why I don't like talking to people. They get all hung up on minor details."

"*Minor details?*"

I don't respond. Talia huffs and stomps along with hands clenched at her sides.

The gryphons lead us around the outside edge of the great Pit to the opposite side where the aerie rises up in tiers. There are very narrow, steep stairs leading from one tier to the next. Just a select few use them since the gryphons simply fly from level to level, and the only ones allowed into the aerie apart from the gryphons are honored guests.

Or those seeking asylum.

While the gryphons leap with the downstroke of their mighty wings to reach the next level up, Talia and I trail behind on the disused steps. Bakari waits at the top of each staircase for us to ascend before leading on. We climb four tiers before halting. Under the unflinching stare of their general, the gryphons currently occupying the space either take flight or leap to a different level until it's just us, the general, and a contingent posted near the stairs as guards.

The general approaches and stops a few feet shy of us. He mantles his wings with feathers ruffled like a bird of prey defending its nest. His might and girth are impressive, always have been. No matter how long I've known him, he remains capable of making me feel very small.

"Under the protection of granted sanctuary," he says, "we will defend you against all hostile forces. However, should your own actions endanger those who shield you, the protection of sanctuary will be lifted."

Talia and I nod in unison. It's the respectful thing to do.

"Why have you come here?" he continues. "Why do the pair of you seek sanctuary with my kin?"

Talia bristles beside me and I fight the urge to roll my eyes.

"She's not with me," I say flatly.

The faun gives an indifferent huff and angles her body to give me the cold shoulder.

One of the guards, the bright golden one that lifted us out of the Pit, steps forward.

"He said the IMS has been compromised, general," she says, the lightness of her voice clearly indicating her as a female. I don't recognize her from my earlier years here.

There's a great many clicking of beaks and shuffling of feathers from the gryphons standing guard behind me. At least they seem more agitated by my announcement than my presence. I guess that means they'll give me a chance to tell my side of the story and haven't decided I'm a villain one way or the other already.

"Speak, young one," the general says and looks to me.

Finally. The whole reason I came here.

The words spill out of me, starting with the hospital and Alona's grave warning about impeccable imposters. I tell them everything I know about the mimics, their ability to pass undetected and to change like shapeshifters but also copy memories as well. While I talk, I keep a hand pressed to my side. I'm aware my body sways where I stand and the lights embedded in the cave walls seem too bright, the world too white. I don't remember the last time I ate and with the excitement of the last hour, my magic and energy has been utterly drained. Not only that, but my state of constant alertness from being hunted on the road finally lifts, leaving me bone-weary and exhausted.

I get to the point in my story about the mother and child. The memory of it combined with everything else makes my knees buckle. I slump to the floor. The female gryphon buffets me with a wing so I don't immediately fall over. My head swims and I lose track of where I am and what I'm doing. The world wheels around me. Her wing brushes against my back and braces me to keep me upright.

One of the guards suggests moving me to their infirmary.

I stretch out a shaking hand.

"Wait," I rasp. "I'm not done. I'm fine."

Bakari blinks so slowly at me that both layers of his eyelids are clearly visible.

With my voice going hoarse, I finish my tale of defeating those mimics and traveling here. The gryphons stand still, their eyes on their general who surveys me with keen intent.

"Please," I rasp. "Please believe me."

"And what of your teammates?" the general asks. "What of their supposed deeds? You were not with them when it is said they committed treason."

"They would *never* do such a thing."

"People change, young one. Who is to say what circumstances might have prompted them to aid Dasc in the end? If Phoenix's brother was involved, who is to say what she would have done? What her team would have done to help her?"

"No," I say firmly. "I'm telling you, whatever the IMS has said about them is a lie. I know them better than anyone else. They aren't traitors and never will be."

I can see the doubt in the dour expressions of the gryphons. They're hard to read but I've spent enough time amongst them to know their tells. The tightening around their eyes, the taut feathers around their beaks.

"*Please*," I say once more and my voice cracks this time. "You don't know them like I do. They're . . . they're family. *My* family. We're sworn to protect this world. I'll do whatever I have to in order to prove their innocence and my own. I'd certainly like to think that coming here has in some way already proven that since this is the last place a real traitor would go."

"You've changed," Bakari says softly.

I wait for him to pronounce judgment or share his opinion on my report of mimics. However, he blinks slowly again and turns to Talia. I follow his line of sight and see the faun is shaking where she stands. I hadn't paid her any attention when

I told my own story but now she looks like she might tremble into pieces. Not from fear, though. No, her hands are clenched tight, long ears flattened, and teeth bared. More like an angry cat than a faun, really.

"And why have you sought us out, child of the forest?" Bakari asks.

"Because my sister disappeared from here three weeks ago," she growls. "I contacted Director Dunham but she refused to listen to me or search for my sister. She's not the first, either. Others of my family have gone missing or …" She stomps a cloven hoof on the ground and the sound reverberates through the aerie. "There was an incident in Underground about a month ago. Two of my cousins and other dear friends died. I was told it was a construction accident. They invited me to come to a memorial. I did. But something felt … *wrong*, so I left. I haven't heard from any of the others that went to that service. Missing. All of them."

Bakari clicks his beak and the other gryphons snort or stamp. "This is the first I have heard of this."

"I came looking for answers," Talia continues. "Everywhere I go, I find more of my friends have disappeared. More than that, I know someone has been following me. This is the only place I could think to go."

"Not Faunus?" I ask. Surely a faun seeking sanctuary would go to a city comprised almost entirely of her own kind.

She gives me a cold side-eye look. "Fauns attempting to travel there are never heard from again. And no one has heard from the city either."

"How have we not heard of this until now?" one of the gryphon guards demands.

I lock eyes with Bakari.

"Mimics," I answer. "It wouldn't be the first time they've spun stories to convince everyone in the IMS of something that's not true."

As to why the fauns are being targeted, I have no idea. Perhaps they aren't the only faction of creatures under attack but we don't know of the others because of the misinformation going around. Or perhaps the fauns know something they shouldn't and are being picked off to hide it. Or perhaps . . . they're somehow a threat to the mimics.

Without a word, the general gestures to the female guard behind me. She nudges me with her beak.

"Stand."

I struggle to my feet and brace a hand on her side to remain upright. She allows the touch and even extends a wing hesitantly as if to catch me should I fall. She also gestures to Talia and the faun takes a step closer.

Then another guard comes from behind to clamp shackles on my wrists and throw a bag over my head.

They don't believe me.

"General!" I shout. "Please, you have to listen to me!"

The gryphons tug me along and I stumble across the rough floor.

"*Bakari!*"

"You killed two innocent humans, not mimics, Charlie."

My heart stops.

"No." The word escapes me on an exhale.

"You will remain here until we can gather the council and pass judgment."

As everything splinters apart, I close my eyes in the darkness of the hood and wish the mimics had killed me at the hospital.

The Past

When the shots go wide left and right, taking chunks out of the fence, and hitting everything *except* the target, my first instinct is to think Phoenix Mason is entirely incompetent. A junior agent that can't hit a target at that distance? How on earth did she ever manage to shoot that werewolf alpha? Was she pressing the gun directly to his chest?

The shakes in her hands are clear. The gun rattles in her grip. She slowly lowers the sights but continues to stare straight ahead. Her brother tries to put a hand on her arm but she shrugs him off and walks stiffly away from us to hide in the barn.

Normally I'd make a scathing comment but the look on Mason's face stops me. His jaw is rigid as he jogs after his sister.

For the short amount of time I've known Junior Agent Phoenix Mason, I've come to think of her as solid with both feet firmly beneath her. Powerful, especially after fighting her in hand to hand combat just minutes before. I've seen her take down a skillful selkie and put a crater in the ground with her fist. She doesn't seem to realize how strong she is. And from all her bravado, I've come to expect more from her. But maybe she's just all talk.

Yet I know that can't be entirely true. I'll admit she's got guts. I guess that's why this seems so out of character. I haven't seen her balk at anything. She was plenty terrified during our car chase after that vampire but she didn't shy away from it. She confronts problems head on—problems like me. I can't count how many times we're argued. Most people give up after a while and avoid me like the plague. But not her.

I shouldn't care. I don't really know either of the Masons well enough to. But when I hear their raised voices coming from inside the barn, I decide to listen in. Walking quickly to the open door, I pause at the base of the stairs, hidden beneath the loft as they argue above oblivious to my presence.

"Don't. Don't do that," Phoenix says. The floorboards creak as she moves back and forth overhead. "I should be able to hit that target consistently. I *used* to. I *can* when I first start but then I—look, I don't want pity. I just want to fix whatever this is. And I don't want you to . . . to think that I regret what I did. I'd do it again in a heartbeat. You know that, right?"

"Is that what you're worried about?" her brother responds. "You think I'll hate you because you're experiencing some form of PTSD for saving my life? For saving everyone? *Piping Pan*, Phoenix. If anything it makes me feel guilty. You were forced into that position and you did the only thing you could in shooting Dasc. There's no shame in that."

"Then why do my hands shake!" she yells back. "Why can't

my stupid brain figure out that I did what I had to and get over it!"

"We'll figure it out."

"I'll never be an agent, Hawk. Not like this. I—I need some air."

Her footsteps come thundering down the stairs. I lean back out of sight but she bolts out the door without ever looking in my direction. Moments later her brother follows. He *does* notice me. Neither of us says anything but he gives me a stony look as if daring me to say something. I don't, and he hurries after his sister.

I remain where I am for a long while, keenly aware that my first impression of Phoenix's shooting ability was grossly unfair. Like my uncle, I was ready to throw away that which I judged not worthy instead of taking a closer look. If Melody had the same attitude about me, I never would have made an invaluable friend.

After several minutes of reflection, I return to training, but the thoughts won't leave me alone.

I don't see much of either of the twins for the rest of the day. When we both end up in the kitchen to eat and use the computers in the loft at the same time, I don't say anything. Phoenix avoids eye contact and keeps her shoulders pulled up. Agent Barnes returns late but doesn't have any news from Duluth.

Eventually, I'm left alone in the barn for the night. I stretch out on the cot in the loft and throw an arm up over my head on the pillow as I stare at the ceiling. The memory of Mason's shaking hands and her words afterwards return to me over and over again. I hate to admit it, even to myself, but I've come to admire some of her qualities, if not her brute stubbornness.

She's like a fire, always smoldering with energy even when idle but the flames come roaring to the surface when stirred. I don't imagine she's one to give up on anything easily.

But I saw her struggling today. A thread of something like . . . sympathy pulls in my chest at that. I know the endless struggle. I've dealt with it all my life. Because of it, I've begun to feel a little guilty about the lies I told her earlier about how I grew up. When people ask that kind of stuff, I tend to keep it simple so I don't have to answer awkward questions. I always say that I'm from Dreamland in Nevada. It was home. I did some work with my uncle. That's it. End of story. But the truth is more complicated and twisted and painful. Although, I did find myself confessing things about my uncle that I'd only told Melody about before. I don't know why.

In the same fashion, I couldn't stop myself from irritating her on purpose while she was working undercover at the school, saying I was her boyfriend of all things. I don't remember the last time I teased anyone without truly meaning it, enjoying it even.

It's only been recently that things have taken a turn for the better. It never would have happened if not for Melody, though. It took someone else's guidance to lead me out of that impenetrable darkness.

At least Phoenix has her brother and Jefferson. They must help in some way. She's not as alone as I was. Still . . . I could say something. Maybe. At some point.

I sigh and roll up into a sitting position. I'm too restless to sleep and my book isn't holding my attention as usual. Deciding to stretch my legs, I rise, throw on my coat, and amble down the stairs. Maybe some fresh air will help clear my head. When I reach the outside door at the bottom of the stairs, I try to open it quietly so I don't disturb anyone in the cabin. The door has other plans and makes a loud, creaking groan.

Startled movement catches my eye.

And there she is. Cheeks ruddy from the cold and red hair in rumpled disarray, Phoenix spins about at the sound of the door. Her hand immediately reaches for her pocket as if going for a hidden weapon.

She looks . . . scared. Eyes wide, face stricken—a far cry from the formidable girl of fury that put a crater in the floor of the barn earlier today. The very same one that saved a town of werewolves and raced after a vampire without hesitation. A ghost of pain is dogging her—it takes one to know one—and I just accidentally hit a trigger reminding her of it.

"I'm sorry," I say and mean it.

She shrugs as if it's nothing to her but exhales sharply and turns away from me to lift her face to the sky full of stars.

Avoidance. Deflection. I bet what's inside is eating her up alive.

I should know.

She probably wants to be alone. If I stay out here, it'll just be awkward and no one wants that. She shivers with her eyes trained on the stars looking lost and hopeless.

I'm not sure what persuades me to move, but I find myself crunching through the snow to walk up to her. She doesn't turn around. There I hesitate, but only for a moment.

"Can I talk to you?" I ask softly.

She turns about with eyebrows raised in surprise. I guess I can't blame her. I haven't exactly been very kind to her, nor anyone really. I'm not even sure myself why I've decided to make contact now. Yet something writhes in my gut seeing the pain she's trying to bury and hide from everyone else. It forces me to move.

"Please," I say.

When I turn back towards the barn she falls into step behind me. We march quietly inside and up the steps to the loft. I move for my cot and gesture for her to take a seat on the table beside it. She slumps like dead weight onto the open tabletop as I sit across from her.

I mull over the right words to say and lean forward on my elbows set on my thighs. Melody knew exactly what to say to pull me back from the brink. It wasn't through pure kindness or polite gestures, but by sharing her own darkness with me, showing me I wasn't alone. It was the first time we connected on a personal level. It made all the difference.

Perhaps I can do the same for Phoenix looking dead-eyed and pale. It's a jarring contrast when I know there's so much more life to her.

I begin, "About four years ago, I went out on my first mission with my uncle. We were tracking a pair of wendigos over in Wisconsin. They had been attacking and eating hikers. You know wendigos, yeah?"

She nods slowly.

"Mind you, this was back when I was inexperienced and absorbed with the heroism of fighting monsters. I'm sure you know what that's like." I raise my eyebrows at her. Considering the enthusiasm I've seen from her when it comes to training, learning about gryphons, and going after that vampire, I can sense we both had the same ideals growing up. We were going to be heroes battling the bad guys like the stories I read as a child. Reality is so much more complicated and ugly.

Her brow creases but other than that, she makes no reaction.

Maybe it was a dumb thing to say.

"Anyway," I continue. "We tracked the wendigos to an abandoned cabin out in the woods along the northern border near Michigan. There was a heap of body parts inside."

I swallow. I can still picture it perfectly in my mind even though I long to forget it. The smell, the blood, the insects buzzing at the pile of flesh. I had vomited. Uncle Laurence admonished me for it despite his own green face and look of disgust at the sight. It still makes me want to vomit.

"I knew we were up against something evil, something unnaturally wrong."

A chill crawls up my spine as I think back on that dark day and shake my head trying to rid myself of the feeling. Of the menacing woods. Of the gruesome carnage left behind by the wendigos. Of the hours spent waiting in terror for the monsters to show.

I force myself to continue. "We waited for the wendigos to return but they were already there watching us from a distance. We fell right into their trap. I won't bore you with the details but I ended up facing one of them on my own. I fought tooth and nail for my life. I managed to stab it with a silver blade right through the heart."

My hand gives a small tremble at the memory of blade meeting flesh and the wendigo's face inches away from my own as it gave one last snarling breath that reeked of rotting meat. And yet in that moment, I felt more terror for what I had done.

I killed a living creature, just as the wendigos did. As if I too was a monster.

"Movies and books make it seem so easy to get past. You kill something evil and you move on. But going through something like that leaves a mark." I'd certainly like to forget it all but the scene surfaces before my eyes from time to time as if to remind me, haunt me. I tilt my head to the side as I suddenly consider that this is the first time I've ever talked about this with anyone. Huh. Well, to the point of my story— "I couldn't go anywhere without a blade after that."

Phoenix is tense across from me and won't look me directly in the eyes. As if I've hit a nerve. Or, hopefully, she's realizing that she's not the only one experiencing that mix of dread and obsessiveness when it comes to a certain weapon. To show that I'm telling the truth, I reach into the pocket of my jacket and pull out the blade I always carry with me. The hilt rolls easily between my fingers and I flip it a few times with practiced ease.

"Still can't, actually. My point is, when you go through something like that everything changes but it's nothing to be ashamed of." Or so I keep telling myself. It's what Melody tells me, too. "It happens. You're the one that shot that werewolf leader, aren't you?"

She keeps her eyes averted. "I didn't actually kill him."

"But it was still a life or death situation, right?"

"Yeah," she says reluctantly.

"Then it's the same thing. Mason, it takes time to sort something like this out. The rest of the world stays the same but you change, and other people just don't get it. Their eyes haven't been opened to the true darkness of reality." I tuck my blade away and finally have her eyes again as if she's waiting for me to go on. "We hunt monsters, Mason. Killing stuff comes with the territory. You've got to accept what happened. You shot a monster. You saved a town. *You* did that. It's done. It's in the past. You can't change it. All you can do is accept it."

She takes a moment studying her hands, several emotions crossing her face in the space of a few seconds. But eventually she tilts her head and her brow scrunches up. Her body relaxes, shoulders sag, and hands uncurl.

"I don't want to change what happened," she says, her eyes unfocused.

I point at her, glad my words seem to have made a difference. "Now *that's* acceptance. But it's only the first step."

"Then what's the next?"

"Retraining your brain to how you react to that event. You've got to dig deep into what that memory triggers. Why do your hands shake when you hold a gun?"

The anger quickly returns to her face. "I don't know! That's the whole point!"

It's an anger built from frustration and denial it seems. I shake my head and hold her gaze. "I don't think that's it. I think you're afraid. The question is, what are you afraid of?"

"I'm not afraid! I—" She stops and freezes up once more, distancing herself mentally again. The distress is obvious in the tightness of her jaw, the shape of her eyes, the creases in her brow. Perhaps I've pushed her too far and she'll completely clam up now. Perhaps I should have been more gentle. I don't really know *how* to be gentle—

"Every time I hear a gunshot I'm back at that night," she says softly. "I wanted to kill him. Sure, I hesitated, but there was a part of me that wanted him to suffer. He killed my parents."

She wets her lips to give herself a moment before continuing. "He's a murderer and in that moment I almost was too. I was a monster, just like him."

An echo of my own thoughts, ones I've struggled with for some time. It's taken years for me to get my head around it.

"I think that sounds like someone saving lives," I say. "Look, when I showed up—in case you forgot, I did show up with the code black squads—your only concern was making sure your brother was okay. And everyone was so grateful you were there to save them. That doesn't sound like a monster to me."

She remains silent and brooding as if she doesn't believe me. Acting on a whim, I invade her personal space without much thought, reach my hand into the pocket of her parka, and pull out the gun I've noticed she always carries around. She doesn't flinch or shy away from the contact. It's almost as if she . . . trusts me somehow. I spin the .45 around in my hands and hold it out to her handle first.

"You drew this when you had to," I say and gently take her lifeless hand to press the grip of the gun into her palm. Again, she let's me do it without any interference or resistance. Oddly enough, that comforts me more than I'm probably comforting her at the moment. "It doesn't fire unless you want it too. You are in control. It's just a tool. If someone came after your brother tonight and using this was your only way to stop them from killing him, what would you do?"

Without hesitation, she whispers, "I'd save my brother."

"Darn right, you would."

She stares at the gun in silent contemplation. From the outside it looks like she's steeling herself as her shoulders raise and her fingers curl around the grip of the gun. I find myself urging her on in my mind, caring more about her state of mind than I ever thought I would. At the same time, guilt begins to chew on my gut as I remember the harsh words I traded with her on a number of occasions when I let my own bitterness get the better of me. Yet here she is and here I am, both spilling our dark thoughts to each other.

I lay a hand over hers and wait for her to look up. She finally does with green eyes clear and vibrant.

"It takes time," I say quietly. "But you've already been facing your fears every time you go out to that range. You've been fighting it all along. You're a fighter. You'll beat this, too. Now, you tell yourself that every time you draw that gun and sight in on a target, all right? You're in control and that gun won't fire until you want it to. We only do what we have to, Phoenix."

I'm suddenly very aware of the weight of my hand on hers and pull back. She draws in a breath as if she had been keenly aware of it too. But then her shoulders pull back, her back straightens, and she doesn't look so troubled anymore. My chest warms. I helped after all.

"Did you just call me Phoenix?" she asks unexpectedly.

I blink. I didn't even notice when I said it, not really. Not wanting to make it a big deal or anything, I puff out of my cheeks and slowly shake my head. "Nope. Definitely not."

"Liar."

She smiles, teasing, and I can't help but smile back.

I don't have many friends. Never have and probably never will. But this right here . . . it feels nice. Funny how the second we stop bickering, we find something in common. I decide I'd much rather be her friend and promise myself to do better.

The thought in itself surprises me and I clear my throat before gesturing to the stairs. "Well, you should, you know, sleep and stuff."

"Yeah, sleep," she says and blows out a sharp breath. "And you should sleep, too. I don't even know why you're still awake."

My eyes automatically dart to the book I left on the bed beside me. I had been reading but other thoughts were what truly kept me awake.

"Or you keep reading," she says. "Whichever sounds better."

I laugh under my breath, glad we've gotten to a point where the words we exchange are now in friendly jest. "Reading always sounds better."

"Well, then." She tucks her gun into her pocket, stands, and walks to the stairs. Before she descends, she says, "Thanks, Charlie."

My eyes widen. It's not often someone's grateful for me or my words. It strikes home then, that I really did make a friend tonight.

"You're welcome."

Present Day
Part 8

No matter how much I rub at my hands, I can't get the feel of blood off them.

You killed two innocent humans, not mimics, Charlie.

I stare numbly at the floor trying not to feel anything at all.

They've locked me in the library tucked behind the aerie. The very same one I used as a refuge years ago, that Bakari himself showed me. The books and curved walls around me were familiar friends when I had none. A place of freedom.

Now my prison.

Part of me wants desperately to escape from here and run to France to find my team.

But there is no escape. Not really. Not from what I've done.

So I sit in solemn penitence waiting for the gryphons to gather the council and pronounce my doom.

Well deserved doom.

They escorted Talia elsewhere so it's just me alone in the library prison. She didn't kill anyone as far as I'm aware so I'm sure she's resting comfortably within the protection of their agreed sanctuary. I hope they figure out what's happening to the fauns and stop it. The mimics must be behind it. But why? I can only speculate. The fauns are not powerful by most standards. They generally don't even know how to fight. They like to grow gardens and dance and be *in touch* with their emotions. And other people's emotions. That's the extent of their magic, really. Empathy. Their greatest—and most irritating—skill.

So why kill or kidnap them? What purpose does that serve?

Wait … Talia had said something felt *wrong* at one point and managed to avoid disappearing like others of her kind. Could it be … the most underestimated of all magical creatures …

The massive door to the library creaks open and heavy footsteps echo through the library. I raise my head. They must have gathered the council already.

It's judgment time.

But it's no gryphon or agent that appears between the shelves with a swaggering, familiar gait. Humor dancing in his eyes, my uncle stalks forward to take up the chair opposite me. He clasps his hands on the tabletop as my heart thunders in my chest. My palms quickly become clammy and the muscles in my neck tense. I can't tear my eyes away from him and his smug smile.

"What are you doing here?" I practically growl.

"Don't you know?" my uncle says and leans in over the table to drop his voice to a whisper. "I'm the one that made you and Team Sierra traitors."

Director Dunham's reliable source.

"After all, Specialist Laurence Jaeger has a lot of pull around here. Something of a legend, really."

My eyes narrow and I angle myself more towards him.

"You're not my uncle."

His smile grows. "Are you sure about that?"

"He doesn't talk about himself in the third person."

The mimic before me shrugs. "True. But I know things only your uncle knows. Say, Charlie, do you still hand wash your shirts in the morning?"

Roaring fills my ears.

He studies invisible dirt under his fingernails as if this conversation bores him.

"Poor me. I joined Team Sierra over in France only to discover they had secret plans to liberate the prison in Dasc's name. During their months of fighting, something in them simply … snapped. To my horror and dismay, I discovered my dear nephew also had a hand in the plot and meant to join them as soon as he had recovered from his grave injury. Such a foolish nephew, who then fled and slaughtered an innocent mother and child that stood in his way. What a tragedy."

My face burns. I can't tell if he's rubbing in that fact or revealing those innocents really were mimics all along.

He sighs dramatically and brushes a hand over the table as if sweeping away dust.

"He despises you, you know. Your uncle." He meets my gaze and I find his eyes pure black through and through. No shred of humanity in that gaze. Soulless, guttering things. "He blames you for what happened to his brother. If only you hadn't been around. Then his brother and sister-in-law wouldn't have fought so much, wouldn't have fought over *you*. His brother might still be alive today running the family business with him. But no. You ruined that dream."

Feelings I had suspected for such a long time. But to have them confirmed by a monster . . . I hide my shaking hands under the table.

"Your uncle only stuck around because of certain advantages you afforded, like letting him remain in this world to train to kill monsters. And your trust fund, of course. He burned through his own money ages ago."

I already know all of this, but it's been a private battle between myself and my uncle for years. To think that this mimic can rip out the memories and use them to his own advantage, I hate it. I hate everything about it.

Then, as if an illusion ripples over him, my uncle's features change until I'm looking at a mirror of myself. The face I've been most dreading to see, for the secrets he'll uncover. My breath catches in my throat.

He—with *my* face, unshaven, green eyes, and all—laughs under his breath.

"So that's what's going on under the hood?" He clicks his tongue, shakes his head, and looks at me sadly. "Charlie, Charlie, Charlie. You're a *mess*. A sad, pathetic mess."

I swallow a few times before I manage to say, "Stop it."

My mirror crinkles his brow thoughtfully and massages the stubble that's nearly a full grown beard at this point.

"So lost. So alone," he says, a perfect replica of my voice. I curl my fingers in the fabric of my jeans to keep my hands from shaking.

"Takes one to know one," I say.

"Bravado." He raises an eyebrow. "But you can only deflect

with it for so long, can't you? You over analyze everything you do, see every flaw, every wrong move, and never let a single grudge go. I'm surprised you haven't committed suicide yet to be honest."

"Shut up."

"But you *have* considered it, haven't you?" My reflection leans over the table with a sinister grin. I didn't even know my face could make such an expression. "More than once. You've thought about taking that one extra step into the Pit in the middle of this city. Sometimes you thought you could push yourself just far enough and simply poof out of existence when you teleport."

My blood boils. Every muscle throughout my body is taut as a bowstring. "*Stop.*"

"Even after being accepted by your comrades and considering them family, you were happy to accept death in Phoenix's place when Epsilon almost killed her." He laughs again and props his chin up in his hand, elbow planted on the tabletop. "She's the one person you'd do anything for. Absolutely *anything*. And still you refuse to admit the truth, even to yourself."

My head swims.

"You love her."

I think I might throw up.

He sighs and traces the grain in the wood with a fingertip. "You don't deserve her, though, and you never will. But you already know that. You'll never confess your feelings because you're afraid she won't reciprocate them. I tend to agree." His eyes bore into my very soul. "How could she ever love someone so pitiful?"

The blow hits deep because the words are straight out of my head. For someone to say it aloud feels like it could break me.

The people I love always leave me. I don't think I could stand it if I lost Phoenix.

You've always had my back, even when I didn't realize it. And when I didn't deserve it.

She left those words for me. I've been holding onto a kernel of hope from what her letter inspired—that there's a chance she feels something greater for me too.

"Too bad that letter of hers gave you false hope," my imposter says.

I glare at my cocky face.

And with a jolt realize I've been glaring at and hating myself for a long time. This mimic has personified all the things I loath about myself and tore open my darkest secrets. I'm falling into a void as the mimic smiles and rips apart everything I think I know. I'm spiraling and I know it. I can recognize when I'm trapped in the sucking mud of my depression. Everything becomes a struggle and it soaks into my bones like heavy, wet sand.

Promise me you'll always keep fighting, and I'll do the same.

His—my—cold laughter fills the room. "I don't even need a physical weapon to gut you. Is this the best the Spartans have to offer? I'm horribly underwhelmed. They might as well leave the fate of the world in the hands of pixies."

I really wish I could hear a snappy retort from you right now.

Her voice fills my head as a distant memory comes bubbling to the surface. It seems like ages ago that Phoenix and I came up against the lamia in Duluth. I made a dumb mistake and was captured. Phoenix and the others came to rescue me. I almost died but she fought for me, carried me on her back, and walked through a blizzard to save me. Even teased that she had kept a little of me close to her heart when she managed to procure a bag of my blood to save me.

I take hold of the memory as if it's a hand extended to pull me out of the darkness.

"I'm surprised you aren't even attempting to fight me," the mimic says. "I didn't realize that gunshot took out your spine, too."

Echoes of Phoenix and Hawk's laughter at the hospital afterwards rings in my ears, of the three of us reading my collection of books. Of our time in Underground during the agent trials. Of our teamwork during Spartan training. Of celebrating my birthday with Team Sierra.

Of Phoenix's whispered words when she curled up beside me on my hospital bed.

I don't want to lose you either.

Moisture wells in my eyes.

"Tears? Really?" His obnoxious laughter fills the room.

Each memory reaches down and pulls me up out of my despair. I cling to every one for the lifeline they offer. I had been alone. But I'm not anymore. I've made unbreakable bonds. I've found a family all on my own. True family.

I level my gaze at the mimc unafraid.

Movement over his shoulder catches my eye—a flicker of flame hovering in midair. I keep my eyes steadfast on the mimic and watch in my peripheral vision as Bakari appears out of nowhere beside the fire sprite, bows his head once, and vanishes once more like a ripple in time and space.

I ease out a breath as I understand.

The mimic rises and dusts off his hands. "Well, as fun as this has been, I have things to do. I am—or rather *you* are—going to thank the gryphons for their hospitality with a *fiery* farewell. We can't risk them actually believing you, can we?"

"I'll stop you."

He holds a hand to his stomach and throws back his head with a booming laugh. "Do you honestly think I'm the only one here? How naive. When we're finished, there won't be anything left of your precious IMS and hidden cities. The Mother rises."

"You're wrong, you know," I say quietly.

He plants his hands on the table and leans in over me. "About what? Our assured victory? You being a good for nothing piece of trash? Your uncle hating you? Or that the girl will never accept your foolish thoughts of love?"

"I'm not lost anymore. And I'm not alone."

"Look around you, Charlie." He spreads his arms wide to the apparently empty room. "You're being held prisoner by the only beings you thought you could turn to for aid. Where are your friends now?"

"Look around you, Charlie," I echo back and slowly spread my arms out to the sides.

As I do, the walls and shelves of books waver. The perception of the empty library vanishes to be replaced by reality. Standing tall amongst the tables and shelves stand rows of armored gryphons. Sprites of all shapes and sizes are spread throughout, the engineers of the grand illusion that had even me fooled. Bakari's sharp glare doesn't move from the fake me whose face has now turned the color of cold porridge.

Bakari never doubted me. No, he saw right through the game and lured a mimic into a trap.

"You said they share memories," the general says without even looking at me. "I couldn't take the risk of telling you the plan in case he would then know."

"I understand." Warmth and relief spreads through my chest. They believed me and I was never alone.

Fake me twists this way and that looking for a way out of his predicament.

It's my turn to smile. "Where are your friends now?"

He launches himself at me. I port behind him, grab his arm, twist it around his back, and slam his face into the table.

"No really," I say. "Where are your friends now?"

He squirms but can't escape my hold. "I'll never tell you, *filth*," he spits. "I hope they string you up and hang you by your guts so your beloved Phoenix can see—"

"That's *enough* of that." From behind a bookshelf Talia trots forward. In a graceful move, she jabs both her forefinger and middle finger to the mimic's forehead.

"*Sleep.*"

He slumps boneless in my hold. The faun nods to me and I let go to find him unconscious. I had no idea fauns could do something like that.

"What can you tell us of him?" the general asks.

Talia rolls her shoulders back, eyes blazing. "Like I said before. They're . . . wrong. I can't sense emotions from them, just a void. A walking, empty shell."

Leave it to Bakari to work out the same thing I did. The mimics were targeting the fauns for a reason and this is why. Even when all else fails to identify the monsters, the fauns can.

"Do you think you would be able to distinguish them from others?"

A moment's hesitation, then a firm nod.

"Then we have a city to cleanse."

The other gryphons surrounding us give mighty war cries in response. Wings shake, feet stomp, and golden armor clinks against each other. Warriors eager for battle.

"Keep him secured," Bakari says and slashes his beak towards the unconscious mimic. "We'll need him to test for weaknesses."

"General." The female gryphon from earlier, the one that saved us from the Pit, steps forward and bobs her head in respect. "The mimic said he was going to give us a fiery farewell. If there are other mimics in the city, they could still be prepared to fulfill an attack against the aerie."

He nods in return. "Keshiana, see to it that a guard is established at all entrances and exits and begin a sweep for any threats in the aerie itself. Take Charlie with you."

I rock back as I stare at the great golden gryphon beside me. "Wait . . . *Keshiana*?"

She makes a cooing sound deep in her throat like she used to as the little gryphlet that once followed me around. "I'm glad I could return the favor in the Pit from all those years ago. I never forgot you, Charlie."

My mouth lifts in a lopsided smile, a mix of relief and joy warming my chest despite what's going on around us.

"The rest of you with me," Bakari says. I stand aside as the gryphons lope out of the library at speed.

Once the group has passed, Keshiana gestures with her talons and I hurry after her. She trots down the tunnel and I'm hard pressed to keep up. I'll be happy when I'm fully recovered from this stupid gunshot wound. Keshiana keeps glancing back at me. She clearly wants to pick up the pace.

"Go," I wheeze. "Warn the others. I'll catch up."

She rushes ahead in a flurry of feathers. As soon as she's free of the tunnel, she propels herself into the air for greater speed. I jog along wincing and pressing a hand to my side. The mimic that came to taunt me took his sweet time. It could be coincidence, or he could have been stalling for others to set a deadly plan in motion. There's a small hope that the mimics couldn't even breach the aerie. The gryphons are very territorial and would have guards on duty at all times. They wouldn't let someone slip by. The taunt of a "fiery farewell" makes my insides squirm. What are the mimics planning? The aerie needs to be secured as fast as possible, and then the rest of the city purged of imposters.

When I finally exit the tunnel, I find the host of gryphons already in action. Many gleam in armor fit to their wide chests and secured behind their wings, smaller interlinking plates protecting their legs, neck, and flank. Golden helmets curve down to a very sharp point in line with the tip of their beaks to be used as both armor and weapon. Gryphons are truly fearsome creatures to behold, especially in such numbers. There are nearly a thousand stationed in Dreamland. Though that number may seem too small for an army, they make up for it in sheer power and prowess.

I pause momentarily to take in the rising tide of gryphons moving into the air. I've never seen them in such a flurry before, even during my years watching them train. The thunder of their many wings drums against my ears.

The mimics don't stand a chance.

"Rally!" Bakari's voice echoes somewhere amongst the gryphons.

Those already in the air swirl round and round like a gigantic tornado, picking up more and more gryphons as they take to the air to join the ranks. I spot Talia near the base of the feathery maelstrom, hands pressed tightly to her sternum as she watches the spectacle unfold overhead.

I walk only a few steps before Keshiana swoops over to me, touching down with her back paws first before settling on all fours.

"I've sent guards to the hatcheries," she says and looks briefly at the circling gryphons overhead, longing in her sharp yellow eyes. "You'll help me check the small passageways that are easier for humans to move through."

"Lead on."

She bounds several feet towards the lower level of the tiers and I follow as best I can.

We hardly even make it to the first of the narrow stairs when two earth-shattering booms rock the ground so hard that I stumble to my knees. Blinding light and rock and dust explode all around. Instinctively I duck and cover my head and neck with my hands. Ear-splitting shrieks of the gryphons make the very air tremble and I can hear nothing else.

When the shuddering of the earth calms, I peer through my narrowed eyelids.

Walls on either side of the aerie have collapsed, great slabs of stone crumbling and falling away, some landing on lower sections of Dreamland. Screams mingle with the shrieks. Burnt feathers float through the air. Thick blood coats the rocks.

Through the absolute chaos, I hear an anguished voice beside me.

"*The hatcheries.*" Keshiana sobs and rises on shaking limbs before shooting into the air straight towards the thickest of the billowing smoke.

The gryphons that survived the powerful blasts scream in agony and fly in droves for the precious chambers where they store and protect their eggs—now scorched holes of smoking stone. I stagger to my feet in a daze and cough away the smoke and dust in the air. Injured and dead gryphons litter the ground. Comrades try to help the fallen. Friends cry over loved ones.

Did I bring this terror upon them by coming here? It's my fault for not moving fast enough, not being in time to stop horrible things from happening *again*.

Those still able-bodied that don't make for the hatcheries let out fierce cries of fury. Normally stalwart creatures, it takes a great deal to make gryphons furious. Now several hundred look intent on murder, their eyes fixated on the areas not crushed by stone below. To the agents crowding in the commons around the Pit. They begin to stalk towards their intended prey, not caring who is and who isn't an imposter. Just hungry for blood and vengeance.

It's going to be a massacre.

"*Stop!*" I shout but my voice is lost in the thundering of wings as the gryphons launch themselves into the people below. There's nothing I can do about the aerial legion taking flight. Nothing but watch in horror.

A gurgled caw behind me draws me back to the wounded. I have some medical training. It's not much but it's something I can do—even though I wish desperately I could do more. A sense of helplessness tries to gut my spirit. But I have to keep fighting in anyway that I can. I take a breath and push the feeling of being powerless aside.

A group has gathered around one particular gryphon. I hurry and shove my way through the crowd of wings to find Bakari lying bloodied on the ground. The breath leaves me. Talia kneels beside him with both hands pressed to his side and teardrops falling on his matted fur and feathers. His breaths are shallow and wet.

His emerald eyes find me. "*Save them,*" he says and coughs up blood. He points a talon and I follow its path to the smoking pit to the east. One of the hatcheries. "Life over blood."

I rest my hand on his bloody beak. He blinks ever so slowly.

Rising to my feet, I gather what energy I can muster and run for the worst of the destruction. I clamber over rocks still hot from the blasts, scrape my palms on jagged edges, and haul myself over huge fallen stones. At last I reach the edge of what had once been a sprawling hatchery only to find it blackened and smoking. Gryphons search frantically for any survivors and dig through the rubble with their powerful talons.

Cracked egg shells and the charred bodies of baby gryphlets are everywhere.

"OVER HERE!" It's Keshiana.

I make out her brilliant golden hues near the middle of the destruction and work my way over to her. She's clawing madly at the ground with two others. Every so often one presses their head into the soil before continuing to dig. When I come close enough, I make out the smallest of holes beneath their talons. A golden egg glimmers in the darkness of the dirt. I drop onto my knees once I'm on the edge of it, dangerously close to the talons scrabbling at the dirt, and offer up my hands to help dig out the eggs buried below. Moving aside loose soil, I realize they've fallen down into a stony crevice that slices deep into the bedrock.

Another boom sounds in the distance. The gryphons cease their digging to perk their feathered ears towards the sound before returning to the task with a frantic energy.

Loose rocks rain from the ceiling. I don't know what's going on out there but it sounds as if Dreamland is collapsing in on itself. We don't have time. We have to get out of this underground deathtrap.

I grab a fistful of Keshiana's feathers at her withers. She snaps her beak so close to my face she almost takes off my nose.

"I can reach them," I say. "I can reach them. Move back."

Her eyes go round and she snaps at the other two before taking a step back. With their deadly talons out of the way, I plant my hands on either side of the hole they made and press my face close to the opening. It's a very tight space between solid rock. The eggs have fallen down maybe ten feet. Even if they managed to widen the hole, they wouldn't be able to reach the eggs.

It's going to be a tight fit. I take a steadying breath.

I vanish.

Okay, I was wrong.

It's a *very* tight fit.

Hardly able to take a full breath and acutely aware of the fact that the rocks could shift at any moment, especially with more blasts going off deeper within the city, I twist about to wrap my hands around the closest golden egg. With some awkward and painful shifting around, I hoist the egg up to the three gryphons peering down at me. They stick their talons in as far as they can go but they're still a good foot shy. Their panicked cries are shrill on my ears.

"Widen the hole as much as you can!" I shout. "I need to be able to see something to port to!"

Talons begin scratching away immediately. Dirt and rocks plink on my back and head while I twist about to bring up as many eggs as I possibly can. Their girth isn't helping the situation. They're as large as ostrich eggs and I can only keep contact with about three at a time, especially with the limited room.

"I'm coming up!" I shout.

Keshiana turns so I can see the glossy feathers of her side. "To me!"

I concentrate on that point. It's not a good angle by any means but it'll have to do. In a blink I vanish and appear topside half crouched next to her foreleg, the eggs shifted to my arms as I willed them to be. One of her companions scoops the eggs straight out of my grip with her wing.

As soon as I'm relieved of my burden, I port back into the crevice and haul out some more. I don't count as I teleport back and forth to deliver the precious few eggs I'm able to salvage from the destruction of the hatchery. I can tell I'm close to a burnout though when I just about faint on the . . . well, whatever number of ports that is now.

"Are you okay?" Keshiana asks and nudges my limp arms with her beak.

Bigger rocks tumble from the ceiling this time when another explosion goes off. In the distance there are cries to evacuate the city, but no alarms like there should be. The mimics must have tampered with those too.

"There's just a couple more," I pant and will the floor to stop rolling like the ocean's surface.

She nods and braces me with her side when I move to look back into the hole, vanishing once more. I'd collapse if it weren't for the walls holding me tight on either side. My shaking fingers clumsily grasp the two remaining eggs. If there were any others that fell in here, I don't see them or they've already been crushed. I haul them up with a groan and then pause there trying to suck down air into my too tight lungs. My head spins, the world blurs, and it's difficult to pinpoint that hole above my head.

Keshiana's eyes draw close to the narrow opening. "Just once more. You can do it, Charlie. One last time."

The earth shakes violently again. The rocks surrounding me press in closer, putting painful pressure on my ribs. Through the muffled earth are even greater sounds of cracking stone. Keshiana flinches above me. The whole place must be coming down.

"I don't think . . . I can," I wheeze. "You should go."

"I'm not leaving you, Strongheart!" She angles herself so I can see her side again. "One last time!"

Eyes watering, I strain to force what's left of my magic to bend space and time. Holding onto the last of the eggs by the tips of my fingers, I let out a cry as I vanish out of the closing trap and to Keshiana's side.

I fall face first into the dirt with the eggs barely held in my grasp.

"Get up!"

It's a miracle I'm still conscious. It'll take another miracle to get me up and moving. A warm beak pushes against my side.

"*Get up!*"

Groaning and gritting my teeth, I somehow manage to push myself up onto all fours. Rocks sprinkle me and a heavier one clips my face just above my eye. Blood streams down and I'm forced to clench my right eye shut. I won't be able to run or port out of here. A warm wing wraps around my back and pulls me in close.

"We fly together," Keshiana says and gingerly scoops up the last two eggs into a single taloned foot. "Climb onto my back."

There's no time for it to really sink in what she's saying and what it means. Each movement a struggle, I pull myself up between the joints of her wings. Leaning low against her neck, I grasp onto either side and try to hold on as best I can with my knees. I rock forward as she dips low. Wings stretch high to either side and we launch into the air with a powerful down thrust. Keshiana's muscles strain beneath me to propel herself faster as the world literally crumbles around us. My stomach lurches with each jarring move and quick maneuver to avoid massive chunks falling from the ceiling. We join a throng of other gryphons desperately trying to escape and make for the Shroud exit at the rear of the aerie.

Dread for the people down in the city coils in my gut, but then I'm too preoccupied with staying on Keshiana's back as she banks at a near ninety degree angle to avoid a rock the size of a small house.

A whirling storm of sprites twists past us and up towards the ceiling. Earth sprites hug the walls trying to hold them together while air, fire, and water sprites do what they can to deflect what falls. They're only delaying the inevitable.

Dreamland is collapsing and will be nothing more than a pile of rubble soon.

Streams of gryphons fly into the long, wide tunnel that leads out to the Shroud. We join the throngs while earth sprites act as supporting columns to keep the place upright. But more explosions echo through the crumbling city. How did the mimics manage to put together such an assault? *No one* noticed bombs everywhere? It makes me wonder how many in the city are mimics. And are they really willing to go down with the rest of us? Or do they have their own escape routes planned?

A ray of light leads us on that grows wider with each passing yard. The exit. Almost there. Gryphons are already soaring out into the opening to escape the deadly trap that had once been their home.

One moment they're free. The next, they're crushed as one last explosion brings the exit down upon itself. Keshiana banks hard and scrapes along the edge of the tunnel before bringing us to a sharp and jolting stop on the floor. Other gryphons ram into us from behind, attempting to stop before they fly headlong into the impasse. Cries of pain, anger, and fear rise once more. I blink away the dust and stare at the massive boulders now blocking our escape. Not one bit of light manages to pierce the rubble.

We're trapped.

Keshiana's screech rumbles up through my legs and into my chest.

I look to the hundreds around us. Great warriors. The mightiest army the world will ever know.

They're all going to die here.

And I'm going to die with them.

Never before has the thought terrified me as much as it does now. It can't end here. Not when I've finally found something worth living for. That mimic may have cut me open to hurt me but he also bared a truth I hardly dared to believe.

The people I love are counting on me.

"Where's the gate mechanism?" I wheeze.

I learned years ago about the emergency iron door set to close the Shroud exit. It's a huge, monstrous thing of several hundred tons. If there's a chance I can get it to slam on the debris, break it apart, and then raise it up in time for the gryphons to escape . . . There's also a chance of it destabilizing the area but it's coming down anyway.

Keshiana leaps back into the air and angles for a doorway along the wall. It's partially collapsed with just enough room for a human to slip through. Keshiana lands directly before it and clicks her beak in dismay. Without a moment to lose, I slip off her back and nearly fall to my knees. I haven't got a drop of power left in my veins and I'm utterly spent. I'll need to do this the old fashioned way. Bracing my hands on the fallen rocks, I maneuver through the tight opening and hallway narrowed by fallen stones. One shift of the rock could crush me. That cheery thought keeps me moving until I reach the gateway control room. Ordinarily it would be large enough for several gryphons but there's hardly enough room for me. And just barely visibly is a small window that looks out upon the outside. An escape route but one only I could use.

I turn away from the hazy view of the active Shroud outside. I won't abandon the gryphons.

The gate mechanism is old school. There isn't a computer guided system, only cranks, gears, pulleys, and massive weights. I grab hold of a large lever using an educated guess as to the right one to release the emergency door, and pull with all my strength.

It hardly moves. I'm not surprised. I try again and again to force it to move. It inches along.

I'm not done yet. I'm not giving up.

I'll fight to the end.

With a mighty roar, I put everything I have left in me into that lever. A groan of metal echoes through the walls like a dormant titan awakening. The crack of rocks shudders through the air. Breathing heavily, I lean against the wall and wait until the sound of it stops before going for the other lever to raise the gate once more. Once I hear it in motion, I stumble my way back out of the control room where Keshiana waits for me, shifting anxiously with the two eggs still clutched in her right talon.

"Was it enough?" I gasp.

"Not enough."

I look towards the fallen exit and see the stones smashed at the top. Pale sunlight leaks through like a taunting joke. But there's no area big enough to allow a gryphon through. Many have already begun digging at what little headway I managed to make, but there's not enough time.

Another trembling explosion sounds behind us and more of the tunnel collapses.

The mimics are going to bury us like the pharaohs of old. Dreamland will be our tomb.

"Can you at least teleport the eggs to safety?" Keshiana asks and extends the two eggs towards me.

I slump against the wall, amazed I haven't simply passed out yet. "I'm dried up. I'm sorry."

"Then this is it. For all of us."

She heaves a sigh and curls up on the ground over the eggs, using herself as a shield in some desperate attempt to save them from the doom racing towards us. Wings folded over herself, she becomes nothing but a mass of feathers.

I did all that I could but it wasn't enough.

My fingers curl around the pendant resting against my chest.

Forgive me, Phoenix. I promise I kept fighting until the end. Now it's your turn to continue the fight.

I should have told you what was in my heart before it was too late.

The world shudders from yet another explosion and I close my eyes.

The Past

The lights, sounds, and smells of the Blue Comet are the same as they've always been. Too dark. Too loud. Too . . . smelly. It does nothing for my mood. It's been foul ever since I discovered Phoenix took a clip of wolfsbane bullets from my uncle. Thinking about it *burns* something deep in my chest. We've fought and argued plenty of times before but this . . . I don't know how we get past this. She and the rest of Team Sierra have kept me going despite the frequent encounters with my uncle. For her to have done this . . .

"You're frowning again," Melody says. She's watching me over her shoulder as she, Alona, and I descend the stairs into the selkie controlled part of the club.

I avoid eye contact and keep walking down the stairs. "Why did you want to meet up here anyway? I thought you hated coming here."

"With everything that's been happening, I wanted to set a few things right," she says. "It's past time I came here. And I . . . I needed some support to come."

Alona nudges her lightly with her shoulder. "We've got your back."

We reach the lower level filled with dancing selkies, mermaids at the bar, strobe lights, and little streams criss-crossing the floor. I remember coming here with Phoenix over a year ago. She—of course—got into a brawl almost immediately. With Melody along, there's a chance there could be another fight.

As soon as our presence is known, the selkies stop dancing and flash dagger eyes at Melody. We pause and wait for her to make the first move. She sighs, glances at us as if to make sure we're still there, and then marches forward to the crowd of selkies gathered.

She starts speaking Gaelic and I glower a bit. I have no idea what she's telling them. Alona looks to me but I shake my head. Whatever it is, the selkies listen without interrupting even once. At first they look angry, but then they become so sad that some actually start crying. It's a tense moment. I remain beside Alona, ready to back up Melody for . . . whatever it is she's doing. I can take a guess, though. After Melody lost her magical skin, she was angry for a long time. She provoked fights with the others and eventually outcast herself despite the fact that she's their princess. I can only imagine she's trying to make amends for the past.

Minutes pass. Melody stops talking. The foremost selkie in the room steps slowly forward then drops to one knee and touches two fingers to her forehead as a sign of respect. The rest of the room follows suit—with the exception of the mermaids who simply look on stunned. The first rises once more and embraces Melody like a sister. As if a collective sigh goes through the room, the others stand, laughter is shared, the music starts up again, and they resume as if nothing had happened. Well, I'm going to assume it went over well.

Melody returns to us with a heartening smile.

Alona harrumphs. "So, are we supposed to kneel or clap?"

"Oh, sorry about that. It was . . ." She blows out a breath and rubs the back of her neck. "I think I need a drink. Do you want a drink? Let's get drinks."

She makes a beeline for the bar and we follow after shaking our heads. After Melody is settled in and we're seated on either side, she briefly explains what happened for our benefit. As I suspected, she was apologizing for her actions earlier that got her banned from this place. She's been embarrassed about it for ages but didn't think she could face her people without friends behind her.

"It's been a bloody nightmare," she huffs and takes a swig of her bright blue drink. "Thank you both for coming. I needed your support."

"We didn't actually do anything," Alona points out.

Melody throws an arm around our pilot's shoulders and pulls her in for a hug. "Oh, just being here was enough."

I stare down at the glass in my hands as I swirl the clear contents around. Simply being there—comfortable silence—had been almost a thing with Phoenix. I'm not great at expressing my feelings for others and neither is she. But someone else's presence, even if they said nothing at all, was enough. To know neither one of us was alone.

"Okay, we're talking about that frown," Melody says.

I look up to find both women staring at me intently. Great. "It's nothing."

They don't stop staring.

"I don't want to talk about it."

Melody starts rapping her fingers on the tabletop. "So . . . what happened between you and Phoenix in Seattle?"

I blanche. "What?"

"She's not here, Charlie. Something obviously happened or she would have come along with you."

"And Theo texted," Alona adds unhelpfully. "Said he's been texting Phoenix for two hours straight. She's really upset about something but she won't say what. Theo said she sounds miserable."

My face burns, my gut sinks, and I return to studying my drink. What am I supposed to say? That she ripped apart any trust we had? Destroyed part of me in the process? I'm angry. I'm hurt. I'm . . . feeling a little guilty about the things I said now, especially hearing how upset she is. But I'm upset too. I have every right to be upset for what she did.

You're a coward. You're just as bad as he is.

I put my head in my hands and run my fingers through my hair.

Melody grabs my left arm and pulls it away from my face. "Stop freaking me out. What happened?"

So I tell them. Phoenix took a clip of wolfsbane bullets from my uncle—of all people—and has been toting it around with her ever since St. Cloud. Alona and Melody confirm that neither of them knew about it either.

"How could she do that?" I say quietly, my voice almost drowned out by the music.

"Did you ask her why?" Alona says.

"No. I called her a coward." I stare at the back of the bar-keep with dead eyes. "I said she was just as bad as my uncle." I swallow. "Then I refused to talk to her after that."

The two women remain silent but share meaningful looks.

"Charlie?" Melody lays a hand on my arm and waits until I meet her gaze. "I don't know what to tell you but . . . you need to talk to her. At least hear her out."

"How can she possibly talk herself out of that one? She took *wolfsbane bullets*. From *my uncle*. Isn't the whole point of—" I glance at the dancers behind us and then lean in close. "She's supposed to be helping them, not killing them."

"As I recall, someone else used to feel that sympathy towards werewolves was an ignorant point of view."

I exhale sharply and drain my drink in one gulp. "*Ouch*, Mels."

"There's always a reason why people do what they do," she continues. "I gave you a chance. Give her one."

"Besides," Alona says. "You two need to get over this if we're going to continue to work as a team."

Like it's something to just "get over." I had put my trust in Phoenix like I'd never done for anyone else—except perhaps Melody. But Phoenix . . . she . . .

I run my hands through my hair again.

I never told her about what really happened that day the horde of monsters descended on Underground. Again, I was up-set with her about her view on werewolves and she refused to listen to me. I wanted to sit with her and Hawk in the stands during the Aetherball Tournament but I couldn't bring myself to do it. I was still angry. Then we were under attack. The ceiling caved in. Monsters flooded the city. And she disappeared in the chaos. I panicked. I couldn't find her anywhere. People were trying to flee but were too injured to make it to the exits. I knew I had to help them but all I could think about was finding Phoenix. I ported people out in droves but I kept going back, not to find more people that needed help, but to find *her*. I ended up getting dragged out when I collapsed from the effort. Then woke up only to find out she had been hospitalized. The shock that gave me almost made me pass out again. I went to see her—I had to—but she wouldn't let me in. I thought hopelessly that she was still angry with me as I had foolishly been with her. I still remember the immense relief when I discovered that wasn't the case.

When my thoughts stray, they stray to her like a magnet. I never knew I could care about someone this way—and yet be so infuriated with them at the same time. When she's around, it's like I'm whole. And when she's gone, part of me is always waiting for her to return. I . . . I don't know what this is or what it means. All I know is that without Phoenix, my world would be rather gray.

And she's the only one now that could cut me as deeply as she did when she took those bullets from my uncle.

Melody and Alona have moved their conversation along to visiting Theo's family again, when Alona's phone rings. She looks at the number, her brow immediately bunches up, and she answers.

"What's wrong?" she says without preamble to whoever is

on the other end of the line. Her eyes grow wide. Maybe eight agonizing seconds go by before she hangs up, launches out of her chair and grabs both my and Melody's arms. "We have to go *now*. Phoenix is in trouble."

My heart stops.

Then I'm in motion. At half a thought, I have us to the stairs, then up, out of the club, and next to the SUV. I don't care if anyone notices. I port into the driver's seat and rev it up as Alona and Melody hop in.

"Who was that on the phone?" I ask as I gun it, tires squealing with my impatience.

"A guardian angel."

"*Who?*"

"We have to hurry," is all Alona says in response. I've never seen her so pale. "She's in Moose Lake somewhere. It's—it's not good."

I can hardly catch my breath. "How bad is this? What's going on?"

"I don't know specifics. Just that we have to get there as soon as possible. Her life's in danger."

I feel lightheaded and run through a stop light before whipping a corner to race for the interstate.

"I'm calling Deputy Graham," Melody says from the row behind me.

Terror saturates every part of me and I weave expertly through the traffic but I can't seem to go fast enough. Fracking crap! Why did we have to come to Duluth when she's in Moose Lake? How are we going to make it in time to save her from whatever's happened? What if's run through my mind. There could be a hydra, or maybe one of those werewolf fanatics. Or . . . oh, sweet majestics. What if the lamia found her? Or she found them? Epsilon had left that horrible taunting message for her on the *Tregurtha*.

I swear, if something happens to her . . . I don't know what I'll do.

I never should have left her alone. I never should have said those things to her. I didn't even give her the chance to explain. My uncle is a manipulative sociopath, I know that. He could have coerced her somehow into taking those bullets. Right now she probably thinks I hate her. I can't let those words be the last thing said between us if—I just can't.

"He doesn't know where she is," Melody says with her cell still pressed to her ear. "She borrowed his car to go look around town but he doesn't know where she went."

"Then tell him to start looking!"

"He already is."

"If she's reminiscing or something, he should try the school. Or that boy's house … dang it, what was his name? Or her old high school friend. The bubbly one. Maybe her parents' burned down house. Or the field office. Or—"

"He knows. I already told him where to start."

My knuckles are white with how tightly I grasp the steering wheel.

Alona puts a hand on my arm. "Breathe. You aren't going to help anyone if you're a panicked mess."

"But she could—"

"Don't do that. We're *all* worried, Charlie."

"I know that," I snap. "But I—"

"But what?"

I clench my jaw shut. I know what I want to say—what I'm thinking selfishly in my head. That I care more than any of them. That their world wouldn't fall apart if Phoenix were to disappear. But mine would. Because . . .

Never did I ever imagine that someone could ever break through the walls I've built, then give me their hand, and lead me out of the darkness. But she has. She is and always has been a spirit of fire. A beacon in the night. A burning sun in a world of gray.

We fly down the interstate. Silence falls with only the loud rumble of the SUV for company. Right as we reach the exit for Moose Lake, Melody gets a call from the deputy.

"Graham? Yes. We're here now. Okay, we'll meet you there." She hangs up and leans forward between the front seats. "He just spoke with Ben and thinks she might be at Ashley's house. We'll meet him there." She passes along the directions and I speed down the country roads.

"Come on, come on, come on," I repeat under my breath over and over again.

Then I see the right address marker and hurtle down a long gravel driveway. Up ahead looms a white farmhouse. It's mostly dark but there are lights on in the lower level. The curtains are pulled aside so I can easily see inside to a barren living room. I slam on the brakes. A woman stands through the window. Not Phoenix. She looks towards me and I immediately recognize that face. It's the lamia that nearly killed me in Duluth, that nearly killed Phoenix.

Epsilon.

She holds a gun but doesn't aim it at us. No, she points the barrel down towards the floor—where Phoenix lies helpless beneath her.

My mother's lifeless body flashes through my mind. Too late. Always too late.

"NO!"

One second I'm in the driver's seat, the next I'm standing before Epsilon at the end of that barrel.

An explosion of sound rends the air and I experience pain as I've never felt before. My body begins to crumple but I reach out and grab the barrel of the gun to try to wrench it away from Epsilon's hand. She hisses and yanks away from me. Before she can fire again, the window shatters and Alona swoops in with a throaty caw. Epsilon ducks and sends a fist into my gut where blood soaks my shirt. My body seizes up, I stagger to the side, and crumple to the ground. A second later Epsilon vanishes. My blood . . . she took my blood. She's gone.

I roll my head to the side and find Phoenix beside me. Eyes open and staring at the ceiling. Unmoving.

"Don't be dead," I rasp, a pleading cry and prayer.

Each breath is a struggle and takes too much effort. But I manage to use my elbows to pull myself towards her and press two shaking fingers to her neck looking for a pulse.

"Don't be dead. Don't be dead."

I don't know if I can feel a pulse. There's too much blood. It's too hard to breathe or think or move. There's only pain.

"Don't be dead. Don't . . . be dead. Don't . . ."

I can feel myself slipping away, like falling into a darkened dream.

If she's alive, then I can accept this. If it means exchanging my life for hers, then at least my life will have meant something.

But if I was too late once again . . .

Then death may be kinder still.

196

Present Day
Part 9

I wait hunched with eyes closed, fingers clenched around Phoenix's pendant, waiting for Dreamland to collapse entirely and snuff me out with it.

The blasts continue but then there's another sound, almost like a mudslide followed by gasps from the gryphons. Light brushes across my eyelids.

I crack my eyes open to beautiful sunlight pouring in through a massive hole in the blockade.

A shout rings through the din. "FLY, YOU FOOLS!"

I know that voice.

The tunnel becomes a flurry of wings as the gryphons don't hesitate to escape through the opening. I can hardly move myself but Keshiana unfurls her wings, grabs me carefully with her talons and sort of slings me onto her back. Despite my limbs refusing to cooperate, I sluggishly manage to get both legs on either side of her torso and hug her neck with the last of my strength.

Then we're off. The wind whips my face and I close my eyes against the cloud hanging in the air. But then bright light presses against my eyelids and I open them to be greeted by open sky. Keshiana soars up into the sunlight with hundreds of her kind. We're momentarily out of the safety and haze of the Shroud.

Down below the ground quakes, buckles, and falls inwards beneath the sand and mountains. I watch the center of Dreamland cave in on itself before the Shroud rises to cover us in a swirling shield of sand and wind. The Shroud grows to envelope us but acts as a wall spreading outwards with the eye of the storm calm so I don't have to worry about inhaling it. I peer over the side of Keshiana's feathers to the ground below. At the very heart of the swirling vortex I spot familiar green scales, shining spikes, and a lashing tail.

"Take me down," I say on an airy breath. "Please."

She dives and I almost go flying over her head. Sensing she's about to send me plunging, she softens her angle of descent and we glide down in gentle circles amongst the hurricane of gryphons in the air. When we near, the dragon's face becomes clear. Every muscle is taut. The fringe fully expanded around her face trembles with exertion. A constant ripple passes through the air before her and vibrates through the sandy ground towards the massive entrance she made into Dreamland. Keshiana lands ten feet away slightly behind the terrene dragon—the only thing currently keeping the exit from collapsing.

"Scholar!" I rasp.

"*Concentrating here*," she growls through gritted teeth.

Keshiana wobbles as the ground shakes beneath her. She keeps her wings aloft and ready to propel us back into the air at a moment's notice. We're not too far from the crack in the ground where gryphons are still streaming out. Some have people grasped in their talons—whether hostages or rescued friends, I have no idea. A troop even have some centaurs awkwardly clenched in their grasp between a few of them.

A trio carry Bakari to safety. I can only hope he's still alive. More wounded are hauled out but the flood escaping slows to a trickle. Those who are able to make it out have. I lean heavily against Keshiana's neck with the weight of the dead at my back. A city's worth of lost souls buried beneath the desert.

The caving ground draws near with increased speed.

"Scholar!" I shout to get the dragon's attention. If she doesn't move, she's going to be sucked down with the rest.

"Not yet!"

"You can't save everyone!" She needs to *move*. "You've done all you can. There's no shame in saving yourself now!"

A couple other gryphons land beside Keshiana and watch the dragon intently as they too sense the impending danger coming for the one who saved them. They inch forward as the yawning pit of earth grows closer every second. Still Scholar holds the escape route open but no one else appears out of the wreckage.

"You have to let go," I say weakly.

She shakes her head and lets out a fierce roar. The cave-in slows its progress towards us beneath the power still rippling out of her. But soon her steadying waves begin to dissipate. Her head sags, a shudder travels down her spine, and she gives a wet cough.

The exit collapses before us.

Just as Scholar collapses to the ground.

The cave-in picks up speed as if it's going to take out half of the mountain.

"Go!" Keshiana yells.

The two gryphons beside us grab Scholar between the pair of them and fly heavily into the sky. We follow swiftly after. I take one last look back at Dreamland, a place that had served as my home for years, before it's nothing but a crater beneath the sands of Nevada.

The world is lost around me and I don't know how far we've flown as I fade in and out of consciousness. Keshiana doesn't let me fall even when my arms and legs dangle limp against her sides. Her lungs are a pair of mighty bellows beneath me. Her wings are steady and sure. At the steady beat of both, I'm lulled in and out of nothingness.

I'm hardly aware when we finally land. I don't have a clue where we are. Just that someone offers me water and a soft place to lie down. When I wake, my fingers are curled around a fistful of golden feathers and a dark ceiling presses down overhead, enclosing me in warmth. I reach up and run my fingers along it, realizing it's a wing. At my touch, it unfurls and a beak clicks above my head.

"That tickles," Keshiana huffs.

Head pounding, I slowly ease about to see her peering down at me with her yellow eyes.

"Thank you," I say hoarsely and give a small bow. "I'm honored." Not only for allowing me the sacred privilege of riding on her back, but the protection and help she's continuously given.

"Honor for bravery, Strongheart," she says and gives a bow of her own.

I swallow, almost too afraid to ask. "How many lost?"

"Too many. But less than what could have been if not for the acts of some." She curls the joint of her wing under my arms and rises to her feet, bringing me with her. "We will mourn. We will survive."

"And my friend?"

She nods and motions with a talon to her back. "I'll bring you to her."

"I'd like to walk with you, if that's all right."

Another nod. She braces me with her wing as I walk on jelly legs. Now up and moving, every hurt sharpens and I notice the bandages on me. In particular, a fat one just above my right eye. I wonder vaguely if I'll have a scar.

Looking up and around, I find we're in an aircraft hanger. Gryphons are everywhere beneath several behemoth jumbo jets that are getting prepped for flight. The back bay doors are open to show the special arrangements made for carrying gryphons. All normal bay side seats have been removed and rubber mats laid down. We must have flown to a nearby IMS transportation hub. In the distance, I see Talia monitoring human personnel preparing the jets for departure.

"What now?" I ask.

"My people will make for the motherland and prepare our forces at our stronghold in Egypt. It is no longer safe for us here."

"Have the mimics come after us again?"

Her eyes slide to mine for a moment. "In a way. I'll show you."

We amble along, my hand on her foreleg and her wing

around my waist. The other gryphons move aside for us. It feels like a terribly long walk to wherever we're going but eventually we slow before a set of rooms lining the hanger bay. Keshiana leads me into one crowded with others of her kind, several eyes darting angrily to a television mounted over their heads with the IMS feeds displayed. My eyes remain glued to it as the footage shows clips of the destruction of Dreamland from the inside. Then, worse, of gryphons attacking people during their flight of rage after the hatcheries were destroyed. Someone had been filming. Someone got that film out. I just barely catch the words of the reporter over the sound of repairs in the hanger behind us.

"We still have not been able to confirm the reason for this unexpected and tragic attack. Contact has been attempted with the gryphon king in Egypt with demands that those responsible for the slaughter of innocents and destruction of Dreamland be turned over to IMS authorities. No statement has been given and the gryphon fleet involved in the attack is still unaccounted for. We ask that all agents be on the lookout and report any sightings of gryphons immediately to the proper authorities."

I sway on the spot. It's only Keshiana's wing that keeps me upright.

"They're blaming the gryphons," I say hoarsely.

"Indeed they are."

I turn at the commanding voice. The gryphons in the room part so I have a clear line of sight to Bakari. His wings are in massive slings, his legs are bandaged, and his feathers have lost their shine, but he's alive.

"General." I give a respectful nod and sag with relief. I thought that maybe he hadn't made it.

"The mimics have done far more damage than I could have

conceived. This battle has thrown our world into chaos but I fear it is only the start. The war has begun, and most of the world isn't even aware of it." He takes a few limping steps towards me. "But you, Strongheart, have earned our eternal thanks for your actions. You and your friend."

"But—" My throat tightens and it's difficult to speak. "They wouldn't have attacked if I hadn't been there. They were targeting *me*."

The gryphon shakes his head. "They could not have orchestrated such an attack with so little time. They meant to bury us long before you ever arrived, but instead, your appearance made them hasty. Only imagine what would have happened if they managed to detonate all of their explosives at once? No one would have escaped. Each of us is alive because of your heroism. We owe you a debt we can never fully repay."

There's a synchronized tapping of talons on the cement floor from the other gryphons in the room.

I swallow back the building emotion in my throat. "So what happens now?"

"Now we prepare and do what we can to undermine the mimics' plans. We will send out our own message and hope there are those who will believe us. I ask you to come with us for your own safety. These foes will surely seek revenge against you for rallying us to the truth."

"I'd like to, general," I say. "But there's a mission I still have to undertake. My team is out there somewhere and they need my help. I have to try to save them before there's no where left to run."

Bakari puffs out his chest. "Whatever help you need, you have it."

"Thank you." My voice cracks and I give him a generous bow.

"I think it best if you see to your friend now," the general says. "There is more to her than you realize."

"What?"

"When treating her, a sample of her blood was taken. She's been tainted by the werewolf disease. There are precious few who are able to exist in such a state and still be able to wield their own magic as she demonstrated. She's no mere terrene."

"I know," I say. The gryphons look like they want to investigate further so I ask, "Where is she?"

Keshiana's wing tightens around me. "I'll bring you to her."

We turn about and head down the row of offices until we reach the furthest one. The second I enter the doorway, there's a clatter of claws and a furry body bullrushes me. I get the breath just about knocked out of me as Ammo collides with my abdomen.

"Ammo!" I give him lavish ear scratches and tummy rubs as happiness alights in my chest. "Who's a good boy? Such a good boy." I look back at Keshiana who's watching me with amusement. "How on earth did he survive?"

"Ran out of the bus entrance before it collapsed. We spotted him when we were scouting for survivors."

I hug him around the neck and he licks my ears. "Thank you for picking him up."

"He wasn't keen on it," she says cooly. "But I remembered your story of how he saved you so we put up with his ministrations. I'm glad he's finally calmed down."

I wince. I'm sure he was barking like mad with all these magical creatures around. Straightening up, my eyes land on the other creature in the room. Scholar is spread out on a pile of blankets in her terrene form, legs tucked in and both her long neck and tail curled around so she's formed a dragon donut. Once I stop petting Ammo, he trots forward right into the little circle made by Scholar's paws and settles in to join her.

I blink. "Wasn't expecting that."

"He's made friends," Keshiana says with a gryphon's smile. "Shall I wait outside?"

"You don't need to wait for me, that's fine."

She bobs her head and stalks out of the room. But the edge of her feathers remain visible just around the edge of the door where she's apparently settled in to guard. A touch of pride and affection for the mighty gryphons grips me. I'll try to be deserving of the title Strongheart they've given me, a very rare honor indeed—one I had only dreamed about as a child.

I limp across the cement floor and ease myself down against the wall to keep myself propped up near the slumbering dragon's head. Her sides work like bellows sending steady gusts of warm air from her nostrils. Her fringe twitches a bit in her sleep like a dog's paws while dreaming. I watch her in silence with my hands resting across my lap. Minutes tick by and I use the time to analyze everything that's happened. The fight ahead is more complicated than ever, but I'm not in this alone anymore. The gryphons will support me in my quest to find and save my team. Scholar will lend her strength too, I'm sure, once she's recovered. We have a plan.

And for now I'm going to enjoy the short bout of rest.

A large scaly eyelid opens and a piercing slit eye finds me.

"Welcome back to the world of the living," I say, adding in an undertone, "Terra."

Her eyes grow wide and she raises her head just so off her forelegs. The fringe flattens around her face.

I give her a wane smile to ease her nerves. "I'm not going to tell anyone if that's what you're afraid of. Although, I think the gryphons might suspect who you really are."

"How long have you known?"

"I suspected for a while." I cross one leg over the other and fold my hands in my lap. "You said you've been searching for a cure for centuries and admitted to being involved in Nymeria's death. That was over five hundred years ago. No terrene lives that long. In fact, no dragon lives that long. Except the majestics. So, that left me with two possibilities. You were either Terra or Eris, the two majestics that *disappeared*—" I mime air quotes. "—after the last great war. But after what I saw at Dreamland, it's clear you're the Worldly Queen. You brought down mountains in your day. Keeping an underground tunnel from collapsing would be a meager task."

"Not anymore," she says quietly and her gaze goes unfocused towards her scarred legs.

"The werewolf disease."

She nods.

I know the horror stories of Blessed being bitten. They never really live after that point. Just survive—if that. The once powerful majestic before me has been simply surviving for the past five hundred years. I can't imagine what sort of agony that must be.

"So, to you, Phoenix is . . . ?"

"A chance," she says softly. "The best chance I have."

The best chance for any of us it seems.

"I need to know what really happened all those years ago," I say and sit up a bit straighter. "If I'm going to help you, I need to know."

"Still don't trust me?"

"It's not a matter of trust anymore." I hold her gaze, lean towards her even as if in challenge. "I can't help you and Phoenix if I'm blind."

She huffs and Ammo's ears perk up as he whines softly.

"I've rarely spoken of such things."

I cross my arms over my chest. "It's time to put your trust in me now."

With a heavy sigh, she snakes her neck my way and lays her head heavily on the blankets nearest me. In a quiet, weary voice she finally explains why she's been in hiding for so long, how she was infected, and her final hopes in Phoenix's blossoming power. I remain silent throughout her story, intent on catching every word. When she finishes, I mull it over and over again in my head. The puzzle pieces connect. The invisible story beneath the surface ties together all the loose ends and everything begins to make sense. Why she's so terrified of Draco.

"History is written by the victors," I muse.

"Not entirely factual, but in this case . . . yes."

"Why not tell the gryphons who you really are? Not everyone is so enamored with Draco."

"That's not the fault of the matter." She huffs another breath that washes over my legs. "I willingly made a pact with Dasc in an attempt to stop Echidna. They would only see me as evil as the monsters I aligned myself with."

It's impossible not to hear the sadness in her voice, the hopeless desperation. I've known the depths of that struggle most of my life. It's as familiar to me as my own reflection. Ammo gets up from his curled position amongst her limbs to lay beside her head and licks a scaly cheek.

"Why are you really afraid to tell them?" I ask quietly. "Because they'll see you as an enemy? Or because they'll confirm your own doubts about the actions you took?"

She swallows and gazes at nothing in particular across the room.

"Through suffering, experience. Through experience, understanding. How strange that someone so small can see so much."

"Reading tends to help, too."

The remark earns a small smile.

"I'm glad Phoenix has you for a friend," she says. "She will need you in the days to come."

Thinking of Phoenix out there somewhere in trouble or pain, twists my insides. My resolve to rescue her and the rest of the team burns like a white hot poker in my chest.

"We're going to save them," I say, my words firm and clear. "We will."

THE ADVENTURE CONTINUES…

Get news about the next book in the series at
brightway-books.com and find exclusive content at
bethanyhelwig.com.

Listen to the playlist that drove the story at
bethanyhelwig.com/book-playlists
Browse the images that gave inspiration for the story at:
www.pinterest.com/phoenixverus/

Bethany Helwig is the author of the successful International Monster Slayers series. She enjoys writing fantasy novels, composing music, creating art, and participating in various fandoms. She lives in a small town in Minnesota with her dog.

Connect with Bethany:
bethanyhelwig.com

TWITTER: twitter.com/BethanyHelwig
GOODREADS: www.goodreads.com/author/show/7152554.
Bethany_Helwig
PINTEREST: pinterest.com/phoenixverus